and
Smell the Coffee!

by

DEBORAH ELUM

All That Productions, Inc.
Humble, Texas

Library of Congress Control Number: 2002093501

ISBN: 0-9679441-4-7

Published the USA by
All That Productions, Inc.
P.O. Box 1594
Humble, Texas 77347-1594

Acknowledgments

I would like to thank my husband, Randy, who always encourages me to pursue the purpose and destiny for my life. To my son, Brian, who always supports, helps, and counsel me with my book projects.

To my mother, Lucy Walker, and father, John Willie Thomas, who gave me their sense of humor and my stepmother, Johnnie Ruth. To my sisters: Carolyn Waldon, Joyce Jones, Gwen Elder, and Jackie Thomas. My brothers: Larry Johnson, Anthony Thomas (A.T.), Ronnie Thomas, and Lynn Thomas. To my sister-in-law, Angelia Elum-O'Neal who has been like a sister to me, and her family, Eric, Eric Jr., and Ms. Renee.

Also, to my friends Ministers Eddie and Kim Torres, Debra Starr, Mary Barnes, Lanie Fenley, Gail Walters, Paula Ferrell, Norma Powers Marlowe, Evangelist Gladys Boggs, and Frankie Lou Arialis. You guys are wonderful.

To my awesome pastors, Roy and Ann Chapman of Worship Tabernacle in Humble, Texas. Thanks to the following great men and women of God who also sowed the word of God into my life; Pastor Patrick T. and Pamela Randolph; Pastor Wilson D. and Ann Douglas.

Mostly, I thank God who inspired me to write my second book, "Wake Up and Smell the Coffee!" God is truly my source!

We're Sisters

Through the pains
And through the gains.
Through the good
And through the bad.
Through the years we all learned
That sometimes we were all that we had.
Through the tears and all the calls,
You've been there for me
through it all.
Worth saying I'm glad
We're sisters.

by
Deborah Elum

Table of Contents

Chapter One
Don't Judge A Book By It's Cover

Georgia Mae and Olivia Faye Nelson were a pair of seventy-five year old twin sisters. They had always been very close. As children, they had spent every waking moment with each other. They did everything and went everywhere together. They were practically inseparable. But somehow through the years, they had grown apart. All the cruel words, jealousy, fault-finding, and complaining had taken a toll on their relationship. Now, they have learned just to put up with each other.

Olivia was about one hundred thirty pounds and stood five feet seven inches tall. She had straight, gray hair that was shoulder length and used a blue rinse to add a little flair. She liked to be in control of everything and everybody. She had given her all to the Lord except her temper which she decided to keep just in case of emergencies. She was the type of woman who did not hold back in giving anyone a piece of her mind. Olivia was set in her ways and determined to stay that way until the Lord called her home.

Georgia, on the other hand, was like a pot simmering on a stove, ready to boil over at any given moment. It took a lot to make her mad but once it happened, she was completely out of control. She stood about five feet four inches and had a stocky build of two hundred pounds. Her hair was black, short, and very curly. She loved to proclaim the good news and the bad.

They lived together in the same house. It was old, but remarkably well-kept. It had a formal living room, dining room, a large kitchen, two spacious bathrooms, and two bedrooms. One of the bathrooms was added on by their mother who got tired of them fighting over who would go first.

Olivia and Georgia slept in the same wooden mahogany bed with a letter carved into the headboard. The letter "E" and another letter which had been obviously chipped out. Neither had ever been married. They had devoted their lives to serving the Lord and aggravating each other.

They were now back to back, shoulder to shoulder, and spine to spine. Each had a firm hold on the small, brown blanket that barely covered the bed. "Stop hogging all the cover," Olivia said as she tugged harder. "You're a selfish old lady. Even when you were a little girl you were selfish."

"And the trouble with you, Olivia Faye Nelson, is that Mama spoiled you rotten."

Olivia sat up and pointed her finger at Georgia. "I've told you a hundred times to leave mama out of it. This is between you and me. And another thing, don't call me by my whole name. You know I hate that." After that announcement she laid back down with her back to Georgia.

"And I hate you giving good people like me a hard time." Georgia pulled harder on the blanket, reclaiming her lost territory. "You're always trying to make me mad, but tonight, I'm not going to take it." She yanked the blanket with all her might.

They each pulled the blanket back and forth like a game of tug-of-war. As Olivia began to pull the blanket, Georgia lost her grip and rolled out of the bed onto the hard wood floor. "Ouch!" she yelled out as she hit the floor like a log rolling down stream. She moaned and rubbed her back. "Oh, my back! Now see what you've done. You made me hurt my back."

Olivia began to giggle when she heard her land on the floor. "You know, the Good Book says that, 'The kingdom of heaven suffereth violence, and the violent take it by force.'" She quickly tucked the extra portion of blanket under her as she lifted up her head to take a peek at Georgia. "Ain't nothing wrong with you so stop faking because you're not going to take advantage of my compassionate nature."

"I'll tell you one thang," Georgia murmured as she placed her hand on the bedrail to lift herself up off the floor, "This bed ain't big enough for the both of us."

"Why don't you go sleep in the chair then," Olivia remarked sarcastically.

Expressing her opinion boldly Georgia boldly stated, "This is my bed just as much as it is yours." She plopped on the bed causing the springs to squeak. *There is more than one way to skin a cat,* she thought to herself. She was willing to use any means necessary. She laid down and turned her back towards Olivia. "I just want to let you know one thang."

"What's that?" asked Olivia hoping for an apology.

"I just wanted you to know that I ate some red beans earlier. You know what red beans do to me. So tonight, I'm going to open fire on you. I'm going to let you have it with both barrels." She pushed several times on her stomach hoping to help the process along.

"Georgia, that's so disrespectful! Don't you dare let out those terrible odors in this room. You go and take some baking soda for your stomach. You should be ashamed of yourself for even thinking such a thing."

Georgia just giggled, laid her head on the pillow, and took hold of what little portion of the blanket that she could. "The only thang I plan to take is my share of this blanket. Here comes the first round." It was not long before the effects could be smelled.

"Oooh, that was terrible," she replied as she pinched her nose. "You know that gas should be bottled and sold to the army as a weapon of mass destruction."

"Well, let go of the blanket and I will stop."

Olivia knew the consequences but she was too stubborn to let go. "Never!" The battle ensued into the early morning hours until Olivia could not take it any longer and began to slowly release her hold. "You can have that old blanket." She threw the cover back, got up out of the bed, took a sheet out of her cedar chest, and laid down in the overstuffed brown chair. Finally the bombing stopped. There was peace again as both sides declared a truce.

Georgia quickly pulled the blanket over into her camp for the victory. As she was taking the spoil from the battle, she began to sing silently to herself as she tucked it under her feet. *Well . . .I went to Olivia's camp an . . . d I took back what she stole from me, I took back what she stole from me, I took back what she stole from me. Well . . . I went to Olivia's camp and I took back what she stole from me. It's under my feet, it's under my feet, it's under my feet, it's under my feet. The blanket is under my feet.* Both of them drifted off to sleep.

The next day, Georgia was the first one to wake up. She was always cranky in the mornings. *Where's that blanket?* was the first thing on her mind as she looked around for it. To her surprise, it was on the floor. The hard wood floor was the only thing that the blanket had kept warm during the night. She sat up in the bed and began to scratch her hairy legs and yawn. Then, she rubbed her face with the palm of her hand. As she looked at her reflection in the dresser mirror, she could see that the whiskers on her chin had grown back overnight. Most of the pink, jumbo rollers in her head had held their course. She was still looking in the mirror when she noticed that Olivia was now staring at her.

Georgia frowned. "Is something the matter?" She turned towards Olivia. "Why are you staring at me?" She was ready for the wrong response so she could let her have it.

Olivia opened her mouth to answer, but shut it again because she did not want to give Georgia a chance to win the argument from last night. She had come to know Georgia well, and although they were twins, there was a line they learned never to cross with each other. Olivia covered up her head and remarked, "Just let me know when breakfast is ready." She thought to herself, *it's going to take a strong cup of coffee to get me through the morning if I have to look at her while I eat.* Then she giggled quietly as the cover concealed her true emotions.

Georgia slipped on her yellow terry robe and her matching yellow bird slippers and slowly made her way to the kitchen as she mumbled all the way. In her routine she would always fill the coffee-stained pot with her very own blend of coffee the night before. It was important to have a cup as soon as she could.

While the coffee was brewing, she put a pan of biscuits in the oven. Then, she made a pot of grits. As she was stirring them with one hand and pouring a cup of coffee with the other, the telephone rang. The brown rotary dial telephone had hung on the kitchen wall for over twenty years. She set down the coffee pot and picked up her coffee cup. Then she made her way across the room with the large wooden spoon that was full of hot dripping grits and her cup.

She wondered, *who could be calling this early in the morning?* She angrily snatched up the receiver and held it firmly to her ear. Quite displeased by the call she responded, "Who is this?"

"Hello, Mother Georgia. It's me Bennie Mae."

"Oh, hi baby." Her voice quickly changed to a pleasant tone. She laid the wooden spoon on the table and pulled over a chair and sat down.

"What's wrong with your voice?" asked Bennie Mae. "I thought that you were a man when you answered the telephone."

"What do you mean you thought I was a man?" Georgia countered hotly as she twisted up one side of her mouth.

"Well, I mean, uh. Your voice . . . sounded so rough when you answered. Is something wrong?"

"Listen baby, you should know by now that I am not a morning person. Now what do you want?" The conversation began to turn sour again.

"Well, I was calling to see how you are doing?"

"I'm glad somebody is concerned about me. Baby, I'm terribly fair. I slipped down in the tub the other day and my back has been bothering me ever since." Georgia began to rub her back. "If I didn't own this house I would sue somebody. The tub is a dangerous place for a woman my age. And my poor bunions and corns have been hurting me since yesterday." Then she began to rub her feet. "My blood pressure is up this morning and my arthritis is even acting up." She opened the box of donuts that was on the cabinet, took out one, then took a bite out of it. With her mouth full and crumbs falling to the floor, she took a sip of coffee from her cup. Then she continued talking. "You know I think I may have sugar too because every time I eat something sweet, I just feel so light-headed. But other than that, I'm blessed," she said as a piece of donut fell on the receiver then onto her lap.

"Maybe you should go see a doctor for a check-up, Mother Georgia."

"Baby, I'm not going to waste my hard-earned pension check on no doctor to tell me what I already know. Giving me all those expensive medicines so they can get rich off of me. No ma'am. Shoot, I remember when I was young, my mama used roots, herbs, and dirt to cure almost anything." She frowned. "These young doctors don't know nothing." She placed her hand on her chest and continued, "Most of them don't even know how to write their name on a prescription and you think I'm going to trust them with this precious cargo. I don't think so."

Bennie Mae smiled. "By the way how is Mother Olivia doing?"

"How is she doing? I guess she's okay. She's still breathing." She switched the phone to her other ear. "She's still in the bed probably snoring to the tune of *Jesus is on the Main Line*. That's why I can't get a good night's rest. If it's not that she's hogging the cover."

"You two should try to get along."

"Baby, you just don't know what all I have to put up with. That woman is starting to get on my last nerve. Take for instance last night . . ."

"Were you two fighting again?"

"Yeah but it was all her fault. I'm trying my best to get along with her but she's as stubborn as a mule. Last night she tried to kill me."

Bennie Mae said in disbelief, "Now Mother Georgia, I'm sure that she didn't try to kill you."

Georgia now standing and speaking in an emotional defensive tone, "I'm telling ya that she did! She pushed me out of the bed. Now what do you call that? You just don't understand what I have to go through with her. She's always trying to start some mess with me."

"I'm sure it was an accident. You and Mother Olivia shouldn't be fighting like that. Remember what you always told me that it takes two to argue and one person arguing by themselves looks like a fool."

"You are so right, I'm the one with the most wisdom in these matters. And like my mama use to say, 'If you stir up mess, it will stink.'"

"You know that you two could not make it two seconds without each other. I know you love her. Don't ya?"

Smiling Georgia replied, "You're right, baby. My mama use to say that all the time to me and Olivia when we were just girls." She paused then said, "Enough about me. What's going on new with you?"

"Well, I have some exciting news to tell ya but it's a secret."

"Now child you can trust Mother Georgia, your secret is safe with me."

"Well, I'll tell ya if you promise not to tell nobody."

"I promise not to tell a soul. Now what is it child?" Georgia waited with anticipation as she took a sip of coffee.

"I wanted to tell you and Mother Olivia at the same time but . . . I'm getting married."

A silent pause came from the other end. Then Georgia responded. "What did you say?" as she splattered coffee all over her yellow robe. Georgia jumped up from the chair and almost pulled the telephone from the wall. "To what? Uh, I mean who?"

"Willie Ray Johnson. Can you believe it?"

"Willie Ray Johnson! Well, praise the Lor . . .d. Now that's some good news child."

"The wedding is in two weeks and I want you and Mother Olivia to be my bridesmaids."

"Now baby you know dresses are high. Me and Mother Olivia are on a fixed income."

"Don't worry about that mother, I'll pay for your dresses."

Georgia took another big bite out of the donut as crumbs landed on the floor. "Well, you know we will have to have shoes, stockings, and of course a matching handbag. We believe in looking good," she said smacking with excitement.

"I'll pay for that too."

"And you know that we have to get our hair fixed."

"Just let me know how much everything will cost. Willie Ray and I will pay for everything ya'll need. Just remember your promise. Don't tell nobody, but Mother Olivia. Okay?"

"Baby, you know I won't say a word to nobody."

"And there is one more thing, I need for you and Mother Olivia to appear before the Board of Elders next week."

"What for?" asked Georgia as her voice began to tremble with fear.

"You know that before anybody can get married at the church, the bride and groom have to appear before the board. All I need for you to do is just tell them you think that Willie Ray and I should get married.

"Let me check my calendar baby because I think that I'm gonna to be busy that day."

"Why is it every time I mention the board everyone gets scared? I hope you're not."

"Well, uh. Baby, I mean, I'm honored you asked me but the Board of Elders ain't nothing to play with."

"Please don't back out. I really need your support. Just think about how good you will look in that new dress."

"Okay baby, I'll be glad to do it. Well, I've gotta go. I'll talk to ya'll later darling." Georgia hung up the telephone before Bennie Mae could tell her bye.

Georgia burst through the french-style doors, she headed straight for the living room. "Thank you, Jesus! I just want to thank you, Lord!" She flew out of the kitchen with both hands in the air. "Glory! Glory, to your Holy Name! You're a miracle worker, Jesus," she said as she rejoiced and spun around. She began clapping her hands and kept repeating the same words over and over again. "Olivia, Olivia!" she yelled out as she headed for the bedroom. "Where are you?" Georgia was so excited that she did not see that Olivia had already made her way to the dining room and was sitting at the table.

"Georgia, what's the matter with you running around here like a chicken with your head cut off?" she asked as she read her Bible and waited for the coffee to get ready. Olivia had read the Bible from cover to cover at least twenty times and was quite familiar with what it said. Doing it, on the other hand, was another story.

"Olivia, you will never guess who that was on the phone."

"Who?" she asked as she closed up her Bible.

"Take a guess."

18

"I don't want to take a guess."

"You can at least try."

"Okay. Did a certain man finally ask you to marry 'em?"

"You know that if a certain gentleman did ask to marry me he better not call and ask me over the phone. Somebody is getting married though."

"Who?" as Olivia's interest peaked.

"Sorry but I can't tell you. It's a secret." She was so excited that she spun around. "So don't pester me because I'm not gonna tell ya." She made her way back into the kitchen with Olivia on her heels.

"So tell me. Who's getting married? Who is it now?" Olivia began to pour on the pressure. Georgia felt like a pot of boiling water and the lid was about to blow off.

"Come on and tell me." Olivia could tell that she was at the breaking point. "Come on tell me. Come on. Girl, you know you want to let it out."

Then, all of a sudden, the news rushed past her lips and out of her mouth. "Bennie Mae is getting married and she wants us to be in her wedding! Isn't that wonderful."

Olivia joined in the celebration and began to sing, "Bennie Mae is getting married, Bennie Mae is getting married, Bennie Mae is getting married, Bennie Mae is getting married and she wants us to be in her wedding!" Then she suddenly stopped, turned towards Georgia and said, "I just want to know one thing. Why did she tell you first? That don't make no sense," she said as she put her hand on her hips. "I know what happened. She really wanted to tell me first but you pried it out of her didn't ya?"

Georgia walked over, picked up the big wooden cooking spoon and hit it on the table. Some of the grits splattered on Olivia's forehead. "What do you mean by that?" asked Georgia as the conversation took an ugly turn.

She took the spoon from Georgia's hand and began to lick off the grits. "Look, let's not argue today. We've got a lot of things to do."

"Yeah, you're right. This is a special occasion for us." Georgia glanced at her full figure in the full-length mirror hanging on the living room wall. She placed her hands on her hips and said, "You know, weddings have a way of reminding me what a beautiful bride I'm going to make."

Olivia didn't dare respond. She knew that the wrong answer could mean death.

Georgia continued to look at her figure. "Whenever Isaac asks me to marry him maybe we can have a double wedding. You and Riley and me and Isaac. How does that sound? Did you hear what I said?"

Olivia quickly tried to change the subject, "Well uh, image that. Our little Bennie Mae is getting married."

"Yeah," Georgia said, "It seems like yesterday that she was a little girl. You know I've prayed for that child to find a godly man until my eyes had swollen up like two fluffy biscuits with butter. Everybody knows that I know how to get a prayer through. My prayers don't linger around the ceiling. They go right into the throne room of the Almighty. When I call heaven, it's direct. She lifted both hands to heaven thanking God.

"Wait a minute! Wait just one minute. You're not the only one that knows how to pray around here," protested Olivia. "I prayed for the poor child myself. She rubbed her empty belly. You know, all this talk about biscuits is making me hungry."

Georgia slowly lowered her hands. "Let's go in the kitchen and have a cup of coffee. The biscuits should be ready by now."

Olivia took her usual seat by the kitchen window. Georgia poured both of them a cup of freshly brewed coffee. Then, she added a little whipped butter, milk, and sugar to the bowl of grits and set them on the table. "You know that Bennie Mae is one blessed child." She took an oven mit from the drawer and pulled out the piping hot biscuits from the oven and placed them on the stove top. Next, she put the biscuits in a large bowl and placed them on the table also.

"Yeah, she's blessed with everything but . . . you know what I mean."

"Yeah, but looks."

"She got her looks from her mama, Sister Pearle," said Olivia as she reached for a biscuit and placed it on her plate. "The apple don't fall far from the tree does it? Both of them are as ugly as homemade soap."

"Uglier," Georgia agreed as she took a sip of coffee, frowned, and shook her head. "You know I don't like to talk about nobody but she's ugly as sin."

"I thought that poor Bennie Mae would never get married," said Olivia. "Bless her heart. It's a miracle. That's what it is. A pure miracle if I ever heard of one. Willie Ray is a nice looking man, financially secure, and owns his own home. He could have the pick of litter when it comes to women. But he chose our Bennie Mae. Our prayers must have caused God to put a veil over that young man's eyes so he can't see how she really looks. That's the only explanation I can think of. Reminds you of the story of Jacob and Leah in the Bible does it?"

"Sho' do. Like mama used to say, 'He had the wool pulled clean over his eyes.' But you know what, I've never seen an ugly bride before," Georgia stated calmly as she bit into her biscuit.

"Well get ready for your first one," Olivia reassured her. They both began to laugh. "I hope Bennie Mae tries to fix herself up for her wedding. Maybe if she wears some makeup and a heavy veil she wouldn't look half bad."

"Well, maybe Willie Ray has learned one of the lessons of life," Georgia said as she took a sip of coffee.

"What do you mean?"

"Like mama would also say, 'Don't judge a book by it's cover,'" added Georgia.

"Wait a minute. We shouldn't talk about her like that," commented Olivia.

"I know," agreed Georgia as she slowly raised herself from the table, walked over to the coffee pot, and poured herself another cup. "We should be ashamed of ourselves. They both giggled. I have a question for ya, "Why is it ugly people have the most beautiful babies?"

"Just another miracle I suppose," Olivia told her.

About that time, they heard the sound of a car horn. Olivia grabbed the side of her chair and leaned over closer to the kitchen window. She reached over and pulled back the old, faded pink and orange curtains to peek out of the window.

"Who is that?" asked Georgia as she rubbed her tired eyes with the back of her hand. Then she put on her eyeglasses that were lying on the table. "What fool is honking their horn like that?"

Olivia waved her hand to make her be quiet. "Hold up one minute till they get a little closer." As the car sped down the gravel-paved road, billows of black smoke poured from the exhaust pipe and covered the road with black soot. As the car came closer, it was obvious who it was by the frown on Olivia's face.

"Riley ain't it?" asked Georgia as she took a sip of coffee.

James Earl Riley was driving his baby blue nineteen fifty-five Buick Road master with white wall tires. He was five feet nine inches tall with a thin build. His neatly trimmed gray beard with streaks of silver gave him a distinguished look. He was a seventy-two year old widower.

Olivia looked at the clock. "It's just six o'clock! Where can that old fool be going at this time in the morning?" She closed the curtains.

A few minutes later, they heard someone knocking on the back door. "Who's that banging on our door like they don't have no sense," Olivia said as she looked over at Georgia. She slowly got up out of her chair, grabbed a wooden spoon from the kitchen drawer to protect herself, then made her way to the door. As she walked, the boards on the wooden floor gave off a loud squeaking sound. "Who's there?" she said in a grumpy voice as she drew back the spoon.

"It's me."

"Me who?"

"It's me, Riley. Your sweetie pie and soon to be husband. Now, open the door woman and let me in!"

Olivia opened the wood door, and unlatched the screen, only opening it part of the way. Riley grinned showing his teeth and gums. He pulled off his hat and waited for an invitation to come inside.

"I was just passing and decided to stop by," he said as he reached out to grab the screen door. When he tried to kiss her on the check, he felt a sharp blow across his knuckles. Olivia had struck him with the wooden spoon.

"Ouch! Why did you do that?" he asked rubbing his hand. "I just wanted a little sample."

"Like I told you before, you can't have the milk until you buy the cow. So that means no smooching until after we get married." She drew back the spoon for another whack. "Got it."

"Good men like me are hard to find, Olivia. If I were you, I wouldn't hold out too long. Some other woman might steal me from ya."

"Yeah right," said Olivia sarcastically.

He spotted Georgia sitting at the table. "Boy that coffee sure smells good," he hinted as he wet his lips. "It's sure cold out here. A nice warm cup of coffee sure would hit the spot."

"Has a cold front come in?" asked Georgia as she leaned forward.

"Yes ma'am. The weather man said that we might even get some snow later on today." Then he focused back on the conversation with Olivia. "If you let me in, I won't tell the other Deacons that I got a peek of you in your night gown." He giggled and placed his fist over his mouth.

She was wearing her large elephant house slippers and her brown and white elephant print robe. "Come on in here you old heathen," she said as she opened the door wider to welcome him in and held out her hand for his hat and coat. She placed them on the empty chair and took her seat again.

"Yeah, come on in, Brother Riley, and I'll pour you a cup," Georgia offered, sitting on the opposite side of the table.

"Thank you, Miss. Georgia."

"Do you want cream and sugar?"

"No ma'am. I like my coffee and my women the same, black and strong." He reached over and pinched Olivia on the cheek. Olivia blushed like a school girl.

"Where's Isaac?" asked Georgia in a disappointed manner.

Henry Isaac was Riley's altar ego. He was medium in stature, five feet six inches, and on the stocky side. He had long side burns and a bald spot on the top of his head. Isaac was seventy-seven years old. He had been a bachelor all his life and content to stay that way.

"He's waiting in the car. We're on our way to the barbershop but I just had to stop by and see my honey first."

"Didn't you just get your hair cut last week?" questioned Olivia.

"Well, yeah. But . . ."

"All you men do down there is gossip like a bunch of old women," said Olivia.

As Georgia set the cup on the table in front of him she asked, "What's new with you Brother Riley?"

"Well, I've got to have a tune up on my . . ."

Before he could continue Georgia broke rank and took over the conversation.

"Did you hear about Bennie Mae?"

"Hear what?" he asked as he stirred his coffee, took out the spoon, and laid it on the table.

Olivia shook her head giving him a condemning look. "Riley you're as bad as Georgia."

"I like information just as much as the next person," Riley admitted as he defended himself.

Georgia rolled her eyes at Olivia. "Well, I don't know if I should tell ya since Olivia thinks it would be gossiping. Besides, Bennie Mae told me not to tell nobody." She paused, looked around, and stared straight into his dark-brown eyes. "You're not a no-body are you?"

He leaned forward. "Of course not. I'm a some-body."

"Well in that case, I can tell ya." She leaned closer to Riley and reported, "She's getting married. Now see there, Brother Riley, you shouldn't have pressured me. You know how hard it is for me to keep a secret. I guess that I let the cat out of the bag."

"You not only let the cat out but the dog too," Olivia said sarcastically.

Riley was in disbelief. "You mean cross-eyed Bennie Mae? I wouldn't have believed it in a hundred years if I had not heard it from you."

"Well it's true. I got a call from her this morning. She wants me and Olivia to be her bridesmaids."

"Well, I know one thing. I'm the only man going to walk my woman down the aisle," Riley said sternly as he stuck out his chest and lifted up the coffee cup to his lips to take a sip.

"I'm quite sure Bennie Mae won't mind you and Isaac escorting us ladies down the aisle."

About that time, they heard a horn blowing outside. It was Isaac blowing the car horn and sticking his head out of the car to see what was the hold up. Riley took another sip of coffee as he got up from the table. He grabbed both his hat and coat and slipped them on.

Olivia jumped up from the table and opened the door to let him out. Then she said, "You give your barber more time than you give me. I don't know what's going on down there but I'll tell you one thing when we get married it had better stop." Before he could answer, she slammed the door shut. "Men!" she said as she looked over at Georgia. "Getting a dog is looking better and better."

Chapter Two
Everything That Glitters Ain't Gold

Cleo Thomas put his key in the door lock. As he touched the ice-cold, metal doorknob, a cold chill rushed through his fingers, and up his arm. The old, brown, rusty hinges made a loud squealing noise as he turned the knob and opened the door.

He thought to himself, *One day I'm going to grease ya.* He had promised to fix that same door everyday for the past ten years but never seemed to get around to doing it. He drew in a breath and stepped inside the cold, pitch-dark room. As he inhaled, he could smell the aroma of cheap after-shave lotion, which still lingered in the air. As he took another breath, he said to himself, *I love that smell.*

The room was dimly lit by a small ray of light coming through a hole in the window shade. He quickly located the light switch and flipped it on. As he looked around the room, everything was just the way he left it the night before. Hair shavings were still scattered all over the floor. Magazines were lying open on the coffee table, revealing their torn pages. The shop was in total disarray.

Cleo took out a box of matches from his coat pocket and opened it. Pulling one out, he struck it against the side of the box, and turned the handle on the gas heater to an upright position. As he held out the match to the escaping gas, a large flame burst free from the heater and traveled up the match stick.

"Ouch!" he yelled as he jerked his hand back. "One day I'm going to buy a new heater. As for you my friend, you will be out on the curb."

Cleo just knew how to talk to anybody or anything. People loved to stop by his shop just to talk. He could hold a conversation with a cockroach if it stood still long enough. The heater was no exception.

"Now we're cooking with gas," he said as the heat began to fill the room. He smiled as he held his hands to the heat and rubbed them together. He took off his heavy coat and scarf and placed them on the coat rack.

Cleo was quite handsome. He had a thin mustache and curly locks which extended down to his shoulders. He had a medium build and stood about six foot two inches in height. Cleo was always clean and a sharp dresser. Being a bachelor, he could have any woman he chose. Women were awestruck by his looks and speech. No matter how many beautiful women came knocking on the door of his heart, he never answered. He was determined to wait on the woman that God had chosen for him. Of course, from time to time, he dated a few of them but considered them only friends.

Cleo had been in business for the past thirty years and had done very well financially. Not only that but he enjoyed every minute of it. He knew his calling was to be a barber when he was just four years old. Even then he always seemed to have a pair of scissors in his hand.

Cleo would always get to the barbershop early enough to pray before he opened for business. He leaned over on a chair and grabbed it by the handles as he kneeled down on his right knee.

"Father. Oh Father. It's me Father. It's your child, Cleophus A. Thomas III." He quickly looked around to make sure no one heard him.

"Father. Do you hear me, Daddy? Oh Father. I said it's me, Lord." He looked up towards heaven and continued, "Your humble servant has come to ya Lord with a low heart and a bowed down head. Father, you know my uprising and my laying down, Lord." Like a truck driver with a big rig, he switched his prayer into overdrive. "Well, well, well. You know every hair on each customer's head. I pray that you be with me as I perm each head and cut each strand. Please Lord, help me not to cut out any plugs today. And Lord, when my work down here is finished, let my last breath be the sweetest breath I've ever had. When my tongue clings to the roof of my mouth and I take my rest, don't let my bed be my cooling board."

Then with a calmness in his voice he slowly changed his tone to a soft slow pace. "I want to be where everyday will be Sunday and Sabbath will have no end. Everyday will be 'howdy, howdy' and no more goodbyes. And you will call me to that big golden barbershop in the sky. I'll be satisfied to cut hair using my diamond and gold scissors for all eternity! If it seems right to you Father, then grant your humble child this final request. Thank ya, Lord. Amen."

After he finished praying, he leaped to his feet, grabbed the handkerchief from his pants pocket, and wiped the tears from his eyes. He composed himself and placed the handkerchief back into his pocket. He walked over to the window and pulled up the yellow and white window shades. He opened the window slightly so the gas fumes from the heater would not build up in the shop. Then walking over to the door and flipped over the door sign that read:

Uncle Cleo's Barbershop
If Your Hair is Straight or Tight
Uncle Cleo will Cut It Right!

"Now it's time for the Holy Ghost and me to get down to business." He took a white barber's coat from the coat rack, slipped it on, and tied the strings around his waist. Sitting down in the chair, he picked up a mirror to check his appearance. After noticing a hair out of place, he quickly took the narrow-tooth comb from his back pants pocket, and combed the stray hair back in place.

Cleo was still admiring his haircut in the mirror when the door opened and T-Bone Jones walked inside. T-Bone had cut hair at the barbershop for the past twenty years. He was short and stocky with salt and pepper hair. He was the comedian and troublemaker of the group.

"Hey there, T-Bone. How's it going man?"

"Oooh wee! It must be thirty degrees out there," he said as he took off his thin, bright yellow jacket and hung it on the coat rack. He took his barber coat from the rack, put it on, then he plopped himself on the couch next to the heater as he tried to warm himself.

"The weatherman said that a cold front was coming in today. You're out early this morning. You normally don't make it in until around nine o'clock on Saturdays. Don't tell me they cut your gas off again?"

"Naw man. Not my gas. I paid my gas bill," he said as he rubbed his hands together. "It's my lights that they cut off this time. I may need to borrow your electric heater until they cut 'em back on."

"No problem. You're welcome to borrow it and the hotplate too if you need it."

"Thanks, I appreciate that. I just need to make a few calls before my customers come in." T-Bone picked up the receiver and held it close to his ear. "My telephone is off too. You know, that telephone company just cut off my phone for no reason. I'm only two months behind. I told that lady yesterday that if she even thought about cutting off my phone, I was going to come down there to her office and kick somebody's you know what. Then, all of a sudden, I heard a click. The next thing I knew, the phone went dead before I told 'em what I was going to do. I wished I had gotten her name so I could report her."

Cleo began to laugh. "T-Bone, you can't talk to those people like that. Man, you're a Christian. They may never turn your phone back on."

"I tell you one thing if they don't turn my phone on, I'm going to let them have some of my good, old time religion. I'm glad I'm saved because I've seen the time I would have cussed her out. She almost made me lay down my religion yesterday."

Before he had a chance to finish talking, the door of the barbershop flew open. In walked Riley and Isaac. He could tell it was going to be a busy day. "Hey there, Mr. Riley and Mr. Isaac. Come on in and have a seat," said Cleo. The men responded with nods and handshakes as they both almost simultaneously took a seat in their usual spot.

Cleo asked thoughtfully, "Does anyone want T-Bone to cut their hair?"

"I sure don't," Isaac replied with an attitude as he rubbed his head. "Last time he charged me too much. I shouldn't have to pay full price since I'm bald on the top and only had hair on the sides of my head."

T-Bone hung up the telephone. "Like I told you before Mr. Isaac, whether you have a head full of hair or just one strand, its still ten dollars a pop. We don't give discounts or take coupons. We're not running a charitable organization around here. Some of us have bills we need to pay."

"Well I tell you what, I'll cut it myself before I pay you another red cent."

T-Bone looked at Isaac. He could tell that Isaac had tried to cut it since one side was cut lower than the other. He chuckled to himself. "We'll just have to call you Bozo the clown." Then he picked up the telephone and began to dial another number. While it was ringing he added, "What you really need, Mr. Isaac, is a hair weave. I can fix you right up. Like I always say, 'If you can't grow it, let T-Bone sew it.'" He began to laugh. "You should think about it."

"That's not funny young man. Ain't no fake stuff going in this head. If the good Lord wants me to have hair again, He'll cause it to grow."

"You should at least think about it," he repeated again as he hung up the telephone and moved over to his barber chair. "I have a lot of customers who wear a weave. You would be surprised."

Cleo looked over at Riley and asked, "Yes sir, what can I do for you today, Riley?"

Riley took a seat in Cleo's chair. "Well, give me the usual. Can you trim those hairs sticking out of my ears while you're at it?"

Cleo threw the black barber's cape around his neck. "Yes, sir," he responded as he snapped the cape ends together. "I know my hands are anointed to cut any kind of hair. Can I get an amen somebody?" He picked up a pair of scissors and whirled them around on his index finger with the precision of a old west gunslinger.

"Amen, brother," responded T-Bone as he smiled. "I've got to give it to you, man. Nobody in the world cuts hair better than you."

"Amen," Riley added.

"Old Man Riley, you must have a hot date tonight?" T-Bone asked as he leaned back in the chair and tried to look wise.

"Now son," said Riley, "Don't be dipping in grown folks business. If I wanted you to know that I had a date, I would have told ya." He wiggled around in the chair to show his disapproval of the question.

"What do you need with a woman, Old Man Riley?" he laughed. "You're too old to be thinking about stuff like that. Leave the courting to us young folks."

"Who you calling old? Boy, you're getting too big for your britches. I could teach you a few thangs. You're still wet behind the ears and you are going to try to council me?" Riley leaned over and said, "Let me ask you a question. Do you have a date tonight?"

T-Bone hesitated. "You mean . . . with a woman?"

"Yep, he's still green," add Isaac as he waited for Riley to throw the knock out punch. "Of course he means with a woman young fella. What planet are you from?"

"Well, no sir."

Isaac could not help but laugh. "An empty wagon makes a lot of noise don't it Riley."

"Sho' do. See young fellow, that's why I've got a date tonight and you don't. Your problem is that you can't find a woman if your life depended on it." The men began to grin.

T-Bone set up in his chair and poked out his chest. "I could have a date if I wanted one. I just have been giving the ladies a break. I can have any woman I want."

"I've never seen anybody with a gift of finding the most ugly women in the world. Ya'll remember that woman he dated that had the mustache. That woman was so ugly she needed to put two brown paper sacks over her head." T-Bone quietly sunk down into his chair as all the men began to laugh again.

T-Bone became offended by the comment. "Well, If a man can wear earrings ain't nothing wrong with a woman who has a mustache."

Suppressing a smile, Riley folded his arms. "Well to each his own."

Cleo had just finished trimming Riley's ear hairs when he began to point his scissors at T-Bone and laughed. "I told you about messing with Mr. Riley. He told you a thing or two." Then, he returned to looking over Riley's hair. "If you have a date tonight, you should get one of my Uncle Cleo's love curls. You see, women love it. It's like pollen to a bee. I tell you it drives 'em crazy. All they want to do is to rub my head." He continued laughing. He put down the scissors and reached for the clippers and turned them on.

"Hold up there now. Put those clippers down," Riley said as he pushed Cleo's hand away from him. "Well, a man is entitled to change his mind. I guess it won't hurt to try one of those love curls one time."

Cleo picked up a jar. As he opened it, the pressure from the formula blew the lid over to the other side of the room. Just the foul smell caused some of Riley's hair to straighten out all by themselves.

"What's in that stuff?" asked Isaac caustically. "I hope it don't take your hair out, Riley," Isaac muttered out of the side of his mouth as he covered his nose.

"Mr. Isaac, this stuff is as safe as can be," Cleo assured him while stirring the secret formula.

As he spoke, Coach Parker opened the door to the shop and stepped inside. "Good morning, everybody," announced Coach Parker as he made his appearance known.

"Hey there, Coach," said Cleo.

"Well, well, you mean your wife let you out of the house without her?" T-Bone began to laugh.

"Watch it now," said Coach Parker as he walked over and shook T-Bone's hand. "How soon can you take me, Cleo? I don't mean to rush ya but I have an important errand to make for my wife when I get out of here."

"I'll be right with ya. Just have a seat."

Coach Parker was the basketball coach at Westbrook High School. He was a large man who was about six feet two inches tall and weighed about three hundred and fifty pounds. He was a family man with five children and a very jealous wife.

Cleo looked at him and asked, "Did ya'll win that game last night?"

"Man, we would have if the referee hadn't cheated us." He grabbed his pant legs at the knees, pulled them up slightly, and then took a seat.

Isaac added in his two cents worth. "Man, ya'll lost by sixty points. They whipped ya'll like ya'll stole something. You need to tell those fellows to put the ball through the hoop once in a while. My grandma could have beat ya'll. Ya'll look like a bunch of rookies out on that court."

Riley asked, "Don't ya'll play Fremont next Friday night? You know they're ranked number two in the nation."

"Fremont is ranked number one now because they beat Columbia last week," injected T-Bone, "I feel sorry for you because they're gonna kill ya'll."

"Man, you don't know what you're talking about. We are gonna win that game," he quickly responded. "What are you getting there, Old Man Riley?" Coach Parker asked warily, changing the subject while leaning forward to get a closer look.

"I'm getting me a love curl," he answered as he leaned back in his chair and crossed his legs. "Tell him, Cleo, how women like it."

"I don't mean to brag on my product but this curl draws the women like a bee to a flower." After Cleo had finished combing the formula into Riley's hair, the telephone rang.

T-Bone looked at the caller ID. "Oh no. It's Lulu Jenkins. Don't answer it," he insisted. That's one lady I wished I had never given my phone number to. I tell you the truth, that's one worrisome woman. It seems like she calls up here at least fifty times a day.

"You mean Lulu Jenkins that works at the bank?" asked Isaac.

"Yeah, that's the one."

"I gave her my number once," said Isaac. "She almost worried me to death too."

"Mr. Isaac you're making that up," T-Bone frowned in disbelief.

"No, I'm not! Young girls like older and mature men. Ain't that true Riley?"

"Yelp, they sho' do. I'm already spoken for. Otherwise, they would be at my door step like a swarm of flies." After the telephone had rung twenty times, there was once again peace and quiet.

A few minutes later the telephone rang again. T-Bone looked at the caller ID and picked it up after it read "unavailable." "I hope that it's the light company calling me back. I left them this number."

At this point, Isaac looked over at Riley. "You mean his lights are off again? That's a shame." They both shook their heads and laughed aloud. "His lights and phone stay off more than a broken television set."

"Joe's Rib Shack. Prime rib speaking," T-Bone joking stated. "Okay, hold on a minute. Cleo it's for you," T-Bone said as he handed him the telephone.

Cleo was still laughing as he answered the telephone. "Hello. Hi, Ester. What do you mean you're cooking something special for tonight? No, I didn't forget our date tonight. Is it fried catfish?" He took the handkerchief from his pocket and began to wipe the sweat from his brow. "You know catfish is my favorite. Well, I'll see you tonight. Yeah, I can't wait to see you too. Bye."

As soon as he hung up the telephone, there was another call. "Hello. Cleo's Barbershop," answered Cleo. "Margaret Mae, didn't I tell you not to call me while I'm working. I'll see you Sunday night. Yeah, I can't wait to see you too. What am I doing? You know I'm working. That means I'm working. Yeah, you too. Yeah. Okay. See you then. Bye."

Riley started laughing as Cleo hung up the telephone. "I see you've got your work cut out for you don't ya young fellow. Your schedule is busier than mine."

"Mr. Riley, these phone calls go on all day long. Come on, let me rinse your hair," said Cleo as he smiled. He helped Riley out of the barber's chair and over to the shampoo bowl. As he was rinsing Riley's hair, the phone rang again.

"I'll get it because I know this call is for me," said T-Bone. "I want my gas on today so I can use my fire place tonight." Again he jested, "Joe's Pool Hall, Eight Ball speaking. Hey, there Jackie. Hold on a minute. Cleo it's for you again." He held out the receiver.

"Hey there my little chocolate cup cake. Can you bring my lunch today? Okay, well I'll see you about noon. Yeah, can't wait to see you too." As he hung the phone up he commented, "See, what I mean, this curl draws the women!"

"That curl is nothing compared to a bowl of Blue Bell ice cream," said Isaac. "Have you tried that new Blue Bell Almond Mocha Fudge? That stuff will make you slap your mama. Blue Bell makes the best ice cream in the world. I said in the world."

"Well, you must not have tasted Breyers yet," replied Riley.

"Breyers," he responded with a frown on his face. "Shoot, they can't even touch Blue Bell. I use to work for Blue Bell for over twenty years before I retired. So I know what I'm talking 'bout."

"Is that all? I use to work for them myself for forty years before I retired," add Riley. He pulled up his sleeve to reveal his retirement gift, a long-ago faded gold-plated watch. "But I still say that Breyers is the best."

"Comparing Blue Bell to Breyers is like comparing a Mercedes Benz to a Hyundai." All the men busted out laughing.

The phone rung again. "Cleo, if you need some help with all those women, you just let me know," said Riley as he leaned over to see if he could hear the next conversation.

"Yes sir, Mr. Riley, I sure will," he said as he started to laugh.

T-Bone looked at the caller ID. "It's Lulu again. Don't anybody answer it."

"Why don't you go ahead and talk to her because she's gonna keep calling up here until you do," said Cleo.

"I'm busy. I don't have time to talk to her right now." After the telephone had finished ringing about ten times, there was silence again. "I don't like a woman hounding me." Truth be told, he did like her.

After Cleo has finished rinsing Riley's hair, he dried it with a large white cotton towel. Then gently combed it out.

Isaac smiled. "Riley, I didn't know your hair was that long. It's down on your back. You kind of resemble James Brown with all that hair. You look so good that if you bathe and put on some cologne, I might ask you for a date myself," he said joking.

"Be quiet, Isaac." He laughed and started to sing, "It's a man's world. But it would be nothing without a woman or a girl."

"You two are too much," insisted Cleo as he begin to put some setting lotion in Riley's hair and roll up small sections with some medium spiral rollers. After he had finished rolling his hair, he helped him over to the large commercial hair dryer and turned it on. "That's not too hot is it?"

"It's fine son. If it gets too hot I'll let you know."

While Riley's hair was drying, Isaac took a jar from his coat pocket. "What ya got there?" asked T-Bone as his mouth started to water.

"Pickled pig's feet."

"I love pickled pig's feet," hinted T-Bone as his eyes gleemed.

Isaac pulled one of them out of the jar and began to suck the meat off the bones. The smell of vinegar began to fill the barbershop. "Do you want one?"

"Yes, sir," he implied as he held out his hand.

"Well, your eyes may shine and your teeth may grit, but none of these pickled pig's feet you gonna get." The men began to laugh.

"Did you hear who's getting married?" asked Isaac as he sucked the last bit of meat from the bones and tossed it into the trash can that was beside his chair.

"Who?" asked T-Bone.

Riley stuck his head out from under the dryer beating Isaac to the punch. "Reverend Pearle's daughter is getting married. Can you believe it? I would have never dreamed it in a million years."

"Really?" T-Bone arched a brow in surprise, then lowered it as all the men looked at him. "You mean cross-eyed Bennie Mae? Now if she can get a man, there's hope for any ugly woman." He began mocking how she looked as the other men laughed.

"I want to know who she is marrying," said Cleo as the conversation peeked his interest.

Riley stuck his head out from under the dryer again. "Willie Ray."

"I don't know why you're talking about her like that T-Bone because you use to date her," Isaac added.

The statement seem to draw an angry look from T-Bone. "Yeah, but that was many years ago."

T-Bone tried to change the subject by saying, "Aren't you and Sister Olivia going to tie the knot soon, Old Man Riley?"

"Next month and I hope to see all of you at the wedding?"

"I wouldn't miss it," said T-Bone. I love to attend weddings. Man, I tell you what, that's the best form of entertainment going."

"We are all gonna be there," said Coach Parker. The other men nodded in agreement.

"In a few weeks that honey is going to be mine. If Mr. Isaac would ask her twin sister to marry him we could have a double ceremony."

"I don't know about that," said Isaac bluntly. "I'm not in a rush to tie myself down. So you can put that idea on the backburner."

Cleo began to clean up his area. "I tell you what, Sister Georgia's a good looking woman for her age. There are plenty of men that would like to have a Christian woman like her for a wife. Have you taken her out on a date yet?"

"Yeah. We've been out a lot of times."

"And what did you think of her?"

"I have to admit that I really enjoy her company but she's put me on her hit list. She's ready to get married but I'm not. I have plenty of time. Nobody is going to rush me into making a hasty decision to get married. Marriage costs a lot of money and women are expensive to maintain. They want new hair do's every week. New dresses, stockings, make-up, perfume, toilet paper, and the list goes on and on. Shoot, all I need is five minutes to take a shower, brush my teeth, comb my hair, iron my good shirt, and I'm good to go. No sir, a wife is too much trouble." He stuck out his hand and waved it from side to side.

"I don't know why people waste all that money just to suffer," T-Bone pointed out. "Before you marry 'em they want you to do that mushy stuff like opening the car door so they can get out. I don't understand why they want us to walk way around to the other side. They could be out by that time. That's why the good Lord gave them one of our ribs and not one of our hands so they can do it for themselves. Next they'll want us to go to the bathroom with them and clean them up. They spend all your money and want all your time." He picked up the dirty towels and placed them in a basket. "Yeah man, once you marry them, they'll try to put a chain around your neck like a dog. They want to know where you've been, where you're going, and what time you'll be back. I mean down to the very second. Man I'm telling you, some women will make you weak as water if you let 'em."

The telephone rang again. All the men looked over to see what woman it would be this time.

T-Bone started to pick-up the telephone but changed his mind. "You get it this time, Cleo. It might be Lulu calling from a different phone number."

"Okay." Cleo picked up the telephone. "Hello, Yes, ma'am, Yes, ma'am. Yes ma'am. Hold on one minute. Coach it's for you. It's your wife."

"Hello, Coach Parker here," he said as he tried to save what was left of his manly dignity. "No dear I was not trying to be funny. Yes, dear. Yes, dear. Yes, dear." Then he hung up the telephone.

All the men looked over at him and busted out laughing. "See what I mean," said T-Bone as he lifted up one of his eye brows. "You can't go anywhere without them tracking you down."

"Your wife said that you only got twenty minutes to get home so I suggest you let T-Bone start on your head right now," suggested Cleo.

"Cleo, you're a blessed man," said Coach Parker as he hung up the telephone and walked over to T-Bone's chair. "You own your own business. You got beautiful women clamoring at your door. You come home whenever you want to. . ." He sighed. "Like they say, 'Life is gresener on the other side.'"

"Now wait a minute, Coach. Life may appear greener on the other side but the grass still got to be mowed. It's not like it seems all the time."

"Well, what about all those gorgeous women?"

"I go home to an empty house every night. I know I flirt with them a little but I am not serious about any of them. They are just friends. Besides most of the women I know don't like me, they like my stuff. My house, my car, bank account."

"Yeah, most of them are looking for a meal ticket," commented T-Bone.

"Believe it or not, I haven't kissed a one of them," Cleo added.

"What you say!" remarked Riley. "What wrong with a little smooching?"

"Nothing but if you play with fire you will get burnt. I have to live right before God. Believe me many of them would go further than that. But my soul is more important to me than temporary gratification. There are some who have even tried to buy me stuff or give me their money, but I'm not for sale," continued Cleo. "I could never take advantage of anybody especially a woman."

"I could," T-Bone said in a reassuring tone. "Man, I don't understand what ya waiting for. Single woman, especially the ones that go to church, if they even think you are interested in marriage, you don't have to cook a meal, iron clothes, or clean your house for the rest of your life. Man, you're sitting on a gold mine!"

"I'm looking for that special woman that the good Lord is going to bring into my life. I'm looking for a women who loves God and is in it for the long haul. That's the one who will be my wife."

"Ahhh, that's special," said Riley as he wiped a tear from his eyes. "I'm nothing but an old softie. Cleo, I'm glad your mama raised you right." He looked over at T-Bone. "It's not what's on the outside that makes a women beautiful but what's on the inside."

"Young man, God is going to bless ya with a good wife you watch and see," said Isaac, "Because you learned that everything that glitters ain't gold."

Wake Up & Smell the Coffee!

Chapter Three
Don't Put All Your Eggs in One Basket

Olivia had almost finished mopping the living room when she heard a knock on the front door. *Who could that be this early in the morning?* she wondered as she placed the mop back in the bucket and headed for the door. The knock got louder and louder. "Stop knocking!" yelled Olivia, "I'm coming."

She opened the door and held it open as two young men made their way inside. "Good morning Mother Olivia," both men said in unison as each hugged her. It was Brother Henry Green and Brother Larry Jones from the church. They would come over once a month to cut the yard, rake leaves, and fix-up the outside of the house when it needed painting.

"You fellows are out early this morning. It's only nine o'clock."

"Yes ma'am we were trying to get an early start because the weather man says it might snow later on today," said Brother Jones.

"Me and Mother Georgia just appreciate you fellows so much for coming over here to rake up all these leaves. We have more than we had last year this time. The Lord's going to bless ya'll for it."

Brother Jones smiled. "It's just a blessing to be able to do it."

"Amen," Brother Green agreed. "It is a blessing. Mother, we are sorry for tracking up your floor."

"Don't worry about that honey," Olivia insisted.

"We'll go through the kitchen if you don't mind," Brother Jones requested.

"Well, okay but you fellows make sure ya'll put everything back like you'll found it when you're finished now. A woman my age shouldn't have to straighten up behind grown folks."

"Yes, ma'am. We will," said Brother Green.

"Cause last time ya'll left out a rack and I stepped on it. I almost knocked myself clean out. And. . ."

While she was still talking she heard another knock on the front door. "Who is it this time?" she said out loud. "Are you fellows expecting anyone else? I don't want a bunch of men hanging around here cause you know how people talk. I have some of the nosiest neighbors in the world," she whispered to them. "I don't want nobody spreading any rumors about me and Georgia. You know we are God-fearing women."

"No ma'am," said Brother Green as he and Brother Jones chuckled. "We're not expecting any-body." The knocking continued.

"Mother Olivia, Mother Olivia. It me, Lulu. Let me in!"

Lulu Jenkins was close to forty-five years old, stood six foot two inches, and weighed two hundred sixty pounds. She could smell a man from a mile away. She had never been married but had everything for her wedding packed away in her hope chest.

Olivia opened the door. "Lulu, what are you doing up this time of morning? You usually sleep till noon on Saturdays."

"I just came over for a cup of coffee," she said as she looked around like a hungry lion looking for its prey. Clearly, she had a lot more on her mind than coffee.

Before Olivia could respond, Lulu pushed opened the screen door and rushed inside.

"Howdy, name's Lou," she said as she tried to catch her breath. But my friends call me Lulu. She pulled off her heavy, hot pink overcoat to revealing her hot pink housecoat. Across her right shoulder hung a large, hot green, plastic, overstuffed purse. Most of her big pink jumbo rollers were still loosely clinging to her head. She had not finished putting on her makeup because one of her false eyelashes was coming unglued and was dangling down across her eyelid.

As Brother Jones reached out his hand to shake hers, she pulled him closer to her and gave him a bear hug. "Ma'am, I can't breath," he said in a high pitch voice. At that point, Brother Green stepped back out of harms way.

"Oh, sorry. I'm just a friendly person. Ain't that right Mother Olivia?"

Before Olivia had a chance to respond, Lulu continued. "I have a wonderful idea." She clasped her hands together, "Let me tell you a few things about me then you can tell me a few things about you. Okay."

Brother Jones said, "Well, Ms. Lulu we got a lot of work to do and . . ."

Lulu held out her hand with a slight attitude for him to stop. "It's not nice to interrupt a lady. I'm just thankful that the good Lord let me live these years to be young as I am. The good Lord has blessed me so much that I have my own car, house, and a good job at the bank. I even have some stocks and bonds. I'm a good listener and I loves kids and best of all I'm single. Ain't that right Mother Olivia." She did not stop long enough for a response. "Oh, I'm sorry I did not mean to let you know that I was single and available," she said with emphasis. "What about you fellows?"

Brother Green was the first to speak. "Well, Ms. Lulu, we both have five kids and . . ."

Olivia reached up and yanked the dangling false eyelash from Lulu's eyelid. "Yeah baby, they are both happily married. These fellows don't play the field like some men I've heard about."

"Ouch!" exclaimed Lulu as she grabbed her eye. She walked over to the coach and plopped down.

"Maybe next time we can bring our family by so you can meet them too," said Brother Jones.

"Well, that's enough talk." Lulu turned her back to them and picked up a bridal magazine that was on the couch beside her and began to look at the pictures in it. Puzzled by her response, both men looked at each other. "Well, mother, we better get started. It was nice meeting you Sister Lulu," said Brother Green.

"Yeah, it was a pleasure to meet you," Brother Jones agreed.

"Yeah, yeah," responded Lulu in a disinterested tone as she loudly flipped the pages.

As the men headed towards the kitchen, they could smell the fresh aroma from the coffee. Olivia said, "Don't forget what I told you fellows," as she pointed her finger at them and squinted one eye."

Olivia turned and looked at Lulu. "I have been cleaning up this house all morning by myself. Every time I almost get through, somebody comes in and tracks up my floor. I'm sick and tired and I don't want anybody else to walk on this floor till it dries. I'm too old to keep mopping the same spot."

"Why don't the church send somebody over here to help you clean up this house?" questioned Lulu as she rared back and propped her feet up on the coffee table. "I know you give a good offering to the church every Sunday. If they keep this up you should stop putting your dollar in the offering plate. So, what do you need done? Maybe I can help you."

"Who are you trying to fool?" snapped Olivia as she took hold of the mop handle. "You didn't come over here to help me clean up. You just wanted to get a look at those fellows didn't you?"

"Why would you say that?" asked Lulu with a guilty look on her face.

"I wasn't born yesterday, baby."

"Mother, I know you. You're not mad cause nobody showed up to help you. You've cleaned this house up all by yourself for years. So tell me what you'll really mad about."

"Child, I can't hide nothing from ya. You know me like a book. It's that sister of mine and that old coon, Riley." She placed the mop back into the mop bucket as water splashed onto the floor. "I'm tired of them provoking me to wrath. Sometimes they makes me so mad that I want to slap both of 'em up side the head." She drew back her right hand and flung it out in demonstration. "Let's go in the kitchen and talk. I just made a fresh pot of coffee."

As they rounded the corner by way of the dining room, they heard the men rush out as the back door slammed shut. As the ladies reached the kitchen Olivia yelled out, "I can't believed it! Those dirty heathens beat me to it." Facing them was an empty coffee pot. "See what I have to put up with. She picked up the empty pot and held it out for Lulu to inspect. Those men are suppose to be raking my leaves not drinking my coffee."

She took out another bag of Georgia's freshly ground coffee mix, put it in the coffee maker, switched the knob to brew, and waited for it to brew up another fresh pot. "Let's sit down until it's ready. Now, where was I," she paused. "Oh yeah, take for instance that old heathen Riley. He's always trying to get a peak at my goodies. But like I've told him before, he can't get a look at the treasure chest until he purchased the treasure."

They had chatted about ten minutes as Lulu shook her head and smiled. "Is the coffee ready?"

"I believe it is baby." Olivia picked up the coffee pot and poured herself a cup. "You want to use one of my cups honey?"

"Mother Olivia, you know that I always carry my own cup." Lulu pulled out her sixty-four ounce coffee stained mug from her purse. "Fill her up," she said as they both began to laugh. Olivia filled it to the brim.

Lulu took a long sip. "Ahhh, this is the best coffee in the world. If ya'll keep this up ya'll are gonna to put Folgers out of business." They reclined back in the chair and began to laugh again.

"Child, your wisdom exceeds your years. You are so right."

About that time Georgia walked in the kitchen, opened up the cabinet door, and took down a clean cup from the cabinet.

Olivia quickly turned around. "Georgia, why are you getting another cup? Why don't you use the one that you used this morning."

"I can't drink out of that cup. I don't know whose lips have touched it since I've been gone. You know I don't drink behind nobody."

"You just want to keep me washing dishes all day. I'm tired of cleaning up behind you."

"I'll wash my own cup then," she said angrily.

Olivia turned her focus back on Lulu. "You know me and Riley are suppose to be getting married in a few weeks. I hope I made the right decision."

"I tell you one thang, he'll have to sleep in the other room because he is not sleeping with me and Olivia," said Georgia. Olivia nodded in agreement.

"Well, do you love him?" asked Lulu.

"Child, men my age are hard to come by. Most of them are buried or should be. I'd better marry him cause some desperate woman might try to snatch him up."

"But do you love him?"

"I hate to admit it but men like Riley are a rare find."

"Do you love him?"

"To answer your question, I do love him."

Georgia remarked, "Like mama used to always preach, 'Don't settle for a slice of bread when you can have the whole loaf.' In Riley's case, a few slices are missing."

Olivia began to frown and look like she had been sucking on a lemon. "Well at least I got a man, Georgia."

Georgia responded by saying, "I guess you're right. A piece of a man is better than none at all." Then she whispered to Lulu and grinned, "Sometimes men his age wet the bed."

While Olivia was taking a sip of coffee she heard the comment. Some coffee went down her windpipe. She coughed, slapping herself on the chest. "What?"

"You heard me." Georgia's grin widened. Maybe she did not win many of the previous arguments of the past, but she could still get a rise out of her sister.

"Not my Riley," she said sternly as she continued coughing. "He has a strong bladder. Lulu, you should have seen him when he was younger." Olivia got up from her chair and walked over to the stove and poured herself another cup of coffee. "What about you, Lulu? Do you want to get married and have a family?"

"Yes ma'am. I sure do. I just can't figure out why it's taken so long for the Lord to send me a husband," said Lulu.

"What type of man are you looking for, baby?" asked Georgia.

Lulu seemed to hesitate before responding. "Mother, I've been waiting so long that I don't care if he's black, white, yellow, or even poke-a-dot. I'm not picky. After waiting for so long, it doesn't matter just as long as his bones don't pop when he walks, and has to have his own set of teeth." All the women started laughing.

"Lulu, you should've been a comedian," replied Georgia. "I know what you mean, baby. My man has to have his own teeth because he's not borrowing mine.

There are three thangs I don't share with nobody, my toothbrush, my false teeth, and my cup."

"Child, you're a young woman. It should be easy for you to find a man," said Olivia as she took another sip from her cup.

"You would think so . . . huh." Lulu traced her finger around the rim of her cup, then looked up. "I don't know what the problem is. I think the Lord needs a little help so I am setting a trap tomorrow for one. I'm going to invite a young man I haven't seen in years over and cook dinner for him."

Georgia said, "So you're getting your ducks in a row. I mean you're getting your plan together. That's good baby because most young woman now days don't know a thang about cooking or cleaning."

"Well, honey remember most men don't think that they need a wife. You have to gently but firmly convince them that they can't live without you. What are you going to fix?" questioned Olivia.

"I don't know. It's been so long since I've seen him I don't even know what he likes. I was hoping to get some ideas from you."

"Well, nothing like fresh coon surrounded by sweet potatoes, squirrel dumplings, or a honey baked rabbit to keep a man happy and satisfied," Olivia said with confidence.

Lulu had a puzzled look on her face. "You know coons today are not like they use to be. Mine comes out tough."

"Baby, coons are too high to mess up. They're almost two dollars a pound!" exclaimed Olivia.
"Tell me how do you get your coon so tender?" asked Lulu.

"Well, its easy," Olivia responded. As she spoke, Lulu leaned forward to understand her instructions. "First, you season the old girl up with salt, pepper, season salt, garlic, and meat tenderizer. Stuff her with some chopped onions, bell peppers, and celery. Then, toss her in a brown and serve roasting bag. Cook the girl slowly on about three hundred degrees for about one and a half to two hours. Those coons be so tender. The meat just falls off the bone. Remember honey, if a woman don't know how to cook a coon, she can't keep no man. Everybody knows that's the way to a man's heart is through his stomach," said Olivia.

"I wonder how Bennie Mae is going to keep a husband then? I know for a fact that she can't cook," Georgia stated as she got up and made her way over to the stove.

"Georgia," said Olivia. "I thought you said that you were going to keep quiet about a certain subject."

"What did you say?" Lulu raised her eyebrows expectantly as she turned her body around to face them.

Georgia poured herself another cup of coffee. "Baby didn't you hear the news?" She hesitated for a few seconds to build the suspense. "Bennie Mae is getting married."

"Georgia," you're like an old broken down refrigerator. You can't keep nothing," said Olivia. "I tell you the truth you can't hold water."

"Hallelujah!" shouted Lulu, "God has lit our fire again." She stood up and began to dance around in a circle and do the moonwalk. "Praise the Lord, hunting season has begun."

"But don't tell nobody that I told you. I'm just the mail man. I just deliver the message. I don't want people to think that I gossip," continued Georgia.

"Too late for that," said Olivia, rolling her eyes. Sarcastically she whispered under her breath, "I guess she's not a nobody either."

Georgia turned and said, "The wedding is in two weeks. She asked me and Olivia to be her bridesmaids. Always a bridesmaid but never a bride." She sighed and took a drink of coffee. "Maybe you should come to the wedding because like mama use to say, 'Don't put all your eggs in one basket.'"

"What does that mean?" Lulu was puzzled by her words.

Georgia eyes widened. "You know there's always lot of single men at weddings. So you can pick out several potential eggs. Got it? Child don't count on just one man."

"Oh, now I got it," she said as understanding had now become clear to her.

"Like mama use to say, 'Don't count your chickens before they hatch,'" Georgia continued.

"That's right, baby," Olivia interjected. "Don't depend on that date to ask ya. I'm sure that there are plenty of young men that's got to be looking for a nice young woman like you."

"You know that if Bennie Mae can get a man," added Georgia, "Your turn can't be far behind. You know there has not been a wedding in the church for over fifteen years. This has got to be a sign from the Lord that the drought is over for both of us."

Lulu was quite curious. "Who is she marrying?"

"Willie Ray," said Georgia as she sipped from her cup.

Lulu's whole countenance changed. For the first time in her life Lulu was speechless. She couldn't believe her ears.

Wake Up & Smell the Coffee!

Chapter Four
God Don't like Ugly

"That's not fair. Not fair at all," Lulu whispered over and over again as she made her way across the street to her house. Hearing the news about Bennie Mae and having to endure life without Willie Ray would be more than any woman could bare.

By the time she got to her front door of her house she was at running speed. The door was still wide open just as she had left it. When Lulu made her way to the kitchen she cried out in a loud voice while stomping her feet, "That's not fair. Not fair at all!"

"Lulu what's the matter?" asked Francis who was sitting at the kitchen table reading the newspaper and sipping on a cup of coffee. "And where's your coat and your purse? Isn't it cold outside?" Lulu had not noticed that she had left her coat, purse, and her coffee mug.

Francis Stern and Lulu were best friends. She would come over every morning to have a cup of coffee and talk about men. She was forty-five years old and stood about five feet two inches and weighed about one hundred and twenty pounds. She was known as the

"Hot Tamale" in the neighborhood because she took stuff off nobody, especially a man. She had been married and divorced three times and was determined to make the next one stick. There are three types of men that she said that she would never marry; a lazy man, a gambler, or a preacher. She had ended up marrying each one of them.

"I loved him first!" cried Lulu as she continued to sob and pace back and forth.

"Have a seat and tell me what happened." Francis got up from her chair and stretched out her hand to help Lulu as they slowly took a seat at the table.

She touched Lulu's arm briefly, wanting to give comfort. "Now tell me what happened. You loved who and what are you crying about?"

"She took . . ." Lulu paused and sniffled, "She took him from me." Lulu began to cry harder.

"Who are you talking about? She took who?"

"Old sneaky, underhanded, low-down, dirty Bennie Mae took my man." Lulu jumped up, walked over, and opened up the kitchen cabinet. She opened it, took a bowl down from the second shelf, and a spoon from the drawer. "I just can't believe it." She took out a gallon of vanilla ice cream from the freezer and placed it on the counter top. She scooped out five big hunks and stuff a big spoonful in her mouth. Over the years, she had spent every available moment scheming how she could hook him and now all her chances were gone.

"Lulu, what are you doing?" asked Francis in disbelief. She then walked over and grabbed Lulu's hand to restrain her from taking another bite. "I thought that you were on a diet." She arm wrestled her hand down onto the cabinet.

"I've just got to have some ice cream or else I am going up beside somebody's head with my fist."

"Well, in that case, have another scoop." She pushed the gallon of ice cream closer to Lulu. "But don't blame me when you want be able to fit in that wedding dress you've packed away for the past ten years."

Lulu began shaking her head and put another big scoop into her mouth. She began to speak but her words were muffled by the ice cream.

"I can't understand a thing you are saying," said Francis.

She gulped it down with one swallow. "It doesn't matter any more because I just found out that Bennie Mae is getting married to my man."

"Girl, you mean Bennie Mae, Pastor Pearle's daughter?" she asked pulling her neck back in shock.

Lulu nodded, seriously, "Yeah that's the one. The old man stealer. She's marrying my man."

"What man?"

"Willie Ray Johnson."

Francis laughed. "What are you talking about Lulu. Willie Ray hasn't been your boyfriend since the ninth grade. Besides, I thought you had your eye on other single men including T-Bone."

"That's not funny," Lulu sobbed. "You know that Willie Ray was my first love. But the old thief stole him right from under my nose." Francis walked over to the paper towel dispenser and rolled off about ten sheets, balled them up, and handed them to her.

"Maybe God put them together, Lou?"

"What?" questioned Lulu as she looked Francis straight in the eyes. No way God couldn't have put her with him," she said, wiping the tears from her cheeks with the rough paper towels.

"How do you know that?"

"Because God don't like ugly." They both started laughing as Lulu continue to wipe the tears from her now puffy eyes.

"Stop being silly and pull yourself together. Now you see that's why I'm not married. Most men ain't nothing but trouble and a big headache," she said speaking from her experience.

"Francis, do you know how long I've been looking and praying that the Lord would get him ready for marriage? About the time he's ready, somebody comes along and snatches him right from under my nose."

"I tell you one thing, I've learned never to put the cart before the horse. I don't count any man as mind, until he puts a ring on my finger and a paper in my hand," said Francis. "When I marry a man this time, I'm going to check out where he works, how much he get's paid, how much he has in the bank, and if he'd doesn't have money to pay off all my bills, I'm scratching him off the list. I'm tired of broke men. And one that don't know how to cook and clean."

"But that ain't right for a woman to take another woman's man," Lulu insisted as she put her head down on the table. "I tell you one thing, I ain't giving him up without a fight."

Francis was quick to respond. "Girl, you know me, I don't believe in meddling in other people's business. And you know that I don't believe in fighting over no man. That man better thank the good Lord for a woman like you. A woman not ashamed to fight for her man."

"Yeah, you're right!" shouted Lulu as she lifted her head and raised her fist in the air. "Ain't no shame in my game. I'm not ashamed to fight for what rightfully belongs to me. I'm going to take my man back. By force if I have to. Two can play at that game."

Francis smiled. "You know that the only one I would fight for would be Reverend Pearle. That man is so good looking that he makes my toes curl up every time I lay my eyeballs on him. He's so nice to Sister Pearle." She walked over and put a scoop of vanilla ice cream in her cup before placing it back in the freezer. "That's one blessed woman."

Francis was right. Reverend Pearle was a very handsome man and built like a body builder. He was about six feet five inches tall and weighed one hundred and seventy-five pounds. He was light complexed with dark wavy hair with light hazel brown eyes.

During Sunday services all the single women would try to sit on the front row to get a closer look at him. They could not wait for service to end so that they could go around and give him a big hug. Some of the married women were even bold enough to wink their eye at him when Sister Pearle was not looking. He knew that they were flirts but he also knew that he loved Sister Pearle and that she was the only woman for him.

"I just want to know one thing. Why is it that the ugly women get the handsome men?" asked Lulu as a tear rolled down her cheek. She lifted her bowl to signal Francis to add another scoop of ice cream.

"I don't know but that's the Gospel truth," said Francis. She put two more scoops of ice cream Lulu's bowl. Then two more in her cup and poured some coffee on top. "I'll tell you what girl, if I wasn't a holy and consecrated woman, I would give Sister Pearle a run for her money." Then she made her way over to the table and took a seat. "I hope she don't act a fool with him because I'm willing and well able to step right on in. If I even hear her say she don't want him, I'm going to sop him up like gravy on a biscuit."

They both started laughing.

After placing her hand on her hip, Lulu told her, "I hope she's not crazy enough to let a good man like him get away. That man is a blessing to any woman."

"Girl, the only way I would have a chance is if she dies. I tell you what, if she even acts like she's dying, I'll snatch him up like buttermilk to cornbread. And I would stick to him like white on rice. That's the kind of man I don't mine waiting on," commented Francis as she crossed her legs and leaned back in her chair.

"Like Mother Georgia says, 'Always a bridesmaid and never a bride,'" Lulu stated as she stood up and place her hand over her heart. She walked over to the kitchen sink. She paused to look out of the window and noticed a car pulling up across the street to Olivia and Georgia's house.

"What you looking at?" asked Francis.

"It's Old Man Riley. He must have made it back. You know that they are getting married. He and Olivia are going to be so happy."

"Yeah, I know. Like I said before, some woman are blessed," commented Francis.

Riley made a call from his cellular telephone. "Hi, baby."

"Hello, Riley," said Olivia. "I can barely hear you. Where are you?"

"Me and Isaac are outside in the car."

"Why are you calling from the car?"

"Well, my sugar dumpling I have a surprise for you so open up the door so I don't have to wait in the cold.

After you do that, keep your eyes closed until I show you the surprise."

She was grinning from ear to ear. "You know I like surprises. Don't keep me waiting too long honey bunch," she said as she hung up the telephone.

"Honey bunch? Who was that?" asked Georgia.

"It was Riley. Who else do you think I would be calling honey bunch?"

"You mean to tell me you're calling him that before you married him? That's dangerous."

"Oh, Georgia, don't be so old-fashioned. The man deserves some type of appreciation since he has a surprise for me. You know how much I like surprises. Unlock the door so he can come in."

Georgia walked over to the front door and unlocked it. "Maybe it's that wedding ring we saw in the window at the Bernardo's Fine Jewelry store."

"Oh, you're probably right dear. I did tell him how much I admired it and that it would make a wonderful wedding ring."

As Riley was turning off his cellular telephone, Isaac said, "I'm not coming in. I'm going to wait for you in the car."

"Okay. I won't be long."

Riley quickly made his way out of the car and to the front porch. He knocked on the front door and then quickly made his way inside. Olivia was there to greet him with stretched out arms, closed eyes, and the biggest smile on her face.

"Okay, you can open your eyes."

After Olivia didn't feel anything in her hands, she opened her eyes and looked down at the floor thinking that maybe the ring had fallen.

Riley stood right in front of her awaiting her response. "You like it?" asked Riley.

"Like what?" she answered as she looked at him.

"My hair. I had it done just for you for our date tonight, pumpkin."

"What in God's green earth did you do to it?"

"Do you like it?" Riley asked again as he began to stroke it. "I got something called a love curl put on it."

"Do you know that singer James Brown?"

"Yeah," spoke Riley enthusiastically.

"Well, you look like his great, great granddaddy."

Georgia had been sitting on the couch and heard the entire conversation. She got up and went over to where Riley was standing. She reached up to feel it. "Riley, it looks good. It's so soft," she said as she pulled out a curl and let it go. "Look, it snapped right back in place. I like it."

Olivia slapped her hand. "That's my man and I don't like it. If you like it so much, have Isaac put it on his head. You better tell whoever did this to you to fix your hair like it was. I mean get that mess off your head quick, fast, and in a hurry. Another thing if you want to surprise me next time it better be with candy, roses, or a big ring. You got it!"

Riley humbled himself and slowly walked out the door. He was a soldier wounded on the battle of love.

Olivia frowned. "Sometimes that man acts like he doesn't have a lick of sense."

"Don't be so hard on him. He did it for you."

"Too bad that he's the only egg in my basket of love," Olivia said as she shook her head. "I see I'm going to have to do a lot of work on him once we're married."

Chapter Five
It'll All Come Out in the Wash

Three Weeks Later

Riley opened the door to the barbershop. "Hey there Mr. Riley and Mr. Isaac. Ya'll come on in and have a seat," Cleo insisted.

"Well, well, look what the cat drug in," said T-Bone as he swept the floor. He sat the broom against the wall and took a seat.

"I didn't get a change to make Bennie Mae's wedding Saturday?" said Cleo. "Man, I had so many customers I had to work until nine o'clock that night. How was it?"

Riley was quick to respond. "Pretty good if you like comedy. Man, I mean to tell you that Bennie Mae rushed down the aisle so fast that she was dragging her poor daddy, Reverend Pearle, behind her all the way."

"Did you see the part when Lulu stuck out her leg and trip Bennie Mae. Unfortunately, she landed on my lap," said T-Bone.

"She sure did," said Riley. "What about the part when the pastor asked if any one objected to the wedding and Lulu yelled out 'I do!' I mean everyone in that place turned around to see who it was. You could have heard a pin drop."

"What happened then?" questioned Cleo.

"Lulu stood up and marched down the aisle. As she marched up the aisle, the music came to a squelching halt. Not only that but Francis and a few other ladies were there egging her on."

"What happened next?" Cleo coaxed.

"Sister Pearle had two big ushers pick her up and throw both her and Francis out of the sanctuary. Lulu was kicking and screaming all the way out, 'That's my man! Bennie Mae you're a man stealer!'"

"You know that Sister Pearle was not going to let her ruin that wedding. It took them too long to get rid of Bennie Mae. Well, T-Bone that means Lulu's all your now," said Isaac.

"I don't think so," said T-Bone. "Like I told you before, I don't like no woman hounding me."

"I can't believe Lulu was capable of pulling a stunt like that. How's that Uncle Cleo Love Curl working for ya?" asked Cleo.

"Well Cleo, you see. Well, uh, I decide to go back to my old hair style."

"What that means is . . . his woman didn't like it," Isaac interjected as he pulled out a pickled pig foot from the jar and began to eat it. "And since they are getting married, he's got to do what she says or she might call the whole thing off."

Riley defending himself. "That's right and you would too if you had a babe like Olivia."

"Well, if you are going to marry her you've got to please your woman," said Cleo in agreement.

"You know, once I was gonna get married," said T-Bone.

"What happened?" asked Riley.

"I didn't tell ya'll about it?" The men shook their heads from side to side.

"Well, I met this woman. Man, I mean to tell you she was fine. I mean she was like my own personal Diana Ross."

"Now that's a fine woman if she was built like Diana Ross," said Riley.

"Sho' is," said Coach.

Isaac laughed. "That woman is nothing but bones." I like a woman with some meat on her bones."

"Isaac you wouldn't know a fine woman if you saw one," said T-Bone as he put his hand on Cleo's shoulder.

"I would too," said Isaac. "Take Oprah Winfrey. Now that's a fine woman."

"Ya'll let me finish," chuckled T-Bone.

"Okay, but I do know a fine woman when I see one," Isaac added, scratching his balding head.

"I mean to tell you the girl had my nose wide open," T-Bone continued.

"How wide was it?" asked Isaac.

"My nose was so wide you could drive a freight train through and still have room left over." The men started laughing.

"But one morning. Say one morning somebody."

"One morning," said Cleo as he hummed it.

"I went over to take her out for breakfast. A woman opened the door and told me to come in. I thought it might be her mother since there was some resemblance. She walked over to a drawer in the living room and took out some fake nails, a wig, body squeezer, false teeth, fake eyelashes, and colored contacts. She went into the bathroom and put them on. When she came back, she took her artificial arm out of another drawer and screwed it on. I just prayed that the Lord would hold her together. Don't get me wrong I didn't mind all that fake stuff but if I had married her I wouldn't know whether to get in the drawer or get in the bed."

Cleo and the men were still laughing when the phone rung. Cleo answered the telephone. "Hello, Cleo's Barbershop. How are you doing? You what?" he said. "Speak up I can barely hear you. What do you mean you don't want your wife to hear you? You and the wife had another fight? Who won this time," Cleo asked as he scratched his head. "Well, you've better get down here right away so I can give you a hair cut and tell you a few things about women." Cleo hung up the phone.

"Who was that?" insisted Riley.

"That was Fred Walker. He had another fight with his wife."

"See, that's why I'm not married. When I go home I don't have to listen to an angry woman," commented T-Bone. "One day that man's gonna learn to keep his mouth shut. You can't out argue a woman. Especially the one you're married to."

"Not all women are like that," comment Coach Parker as he turned the pages of the local newspaper to the sports section.

"Well, if you can show me one that ain't, I'll marry her right now," continued T-Bone as he trimmed the ends of Coach Parker's hair. "I just got one question. Are there any happily married men in the world? Please show me one."

"Of course there are," said Coach Parker. "My neighbor, Mr. Godson has been going to that new church, New Beginnings Christian Center. He told me that his life has changed one hundred and eighty degrees. I'm thinking about going there one Sunday. He said that the pastor and his wife have been happily married for over thirty years."

"What's the pastor's name?" asked Isaac.

"I think she told me it was Pastor Willis."

"Pastor Willis? Shoot, replied T-Bone. "Pastor Willis runs more women then me."

"What! That's not true," said Riley as he scooted to the edge of his chair to get the inside scoop.

"Yep, sho' is," said T-Bone as Coach got up out of the chair and handed him a ten dollar bill. T-Bone sat down in the barber's chair and said, "I saw him pulling in the One Hour or Less Express Motel with the church pianist, Sister Thomas."

He reached over and pulled a straw out of the broom to use as a toothpick. He leaned back in his chair. "And I even saw him smooching with another woman on the way out. He came in with one woman and left out with another. He's a fast worker."

"Are you sure?" asked Riley as he leaned forward like a news man on to a hot tip.

"Before you spread mess around on a man of God you better make sure you are telling the truth," cautioned Cleo. "Sometimes things look one way when in fact it was not true. In other words, eyes can deceive you man. How do you know it was someone else? You know that Pastor Willis has tinted windows in his car. It could have been his wife in the car with him."

"I know what I saw!" T-Bone said sharply as he jumped up out of the chair. "Who in their right mind would spend money taking their wife to a motel when he could take her home?"

Cleo began to rinse the perm remover off of Riley's hair. "One thing about the truth, it's like this perm remover, it will all come out in the wash."

"What does that mean?" asked T-Bone, tilting his head.

"What I'm trying to say is that the truth always comes out."

"Well like they say too, 'When the cat's away, the mice will play,'" Isaac pointed out.

"See people like that is what give Christians a bad name," Riley stated boldly.

"Hand me the conditioner, T-Bone," insisted Cleo as he shook his head and reached out his hand.

"I was trying to get her for myself but the Reverend beat me to her," continued T-Bone as he picked up the conditioner and handed it to Cleo.

Cleo looked out the window and spotted Pastor Willis driving up in his nineteen sixty-four canary yellow Buick. "Hey everybody, be quiet!" Cleo urged and looked out the window again. "Pastor Willis just drove up. He usually comes in on Wednesday."

"Quick," said T-Bone, "Hide your women. No woman is safe around him."

"Well, he can't have my woman. Homey, don't play that," said Riley. Then some of the men burst out laughing.

"What about Old Lady Andrews that lives down the street from me?" asked Isaac.

T-Bone laughed so hard that he fell out of his chair onto the floor.

"Hurry and get up before he comes in here," remarked Cleo.

As Pastor Willis walked through the door, everyone snapped to attention like a captain boarding his ship.

"Hey there Rev," said Cleo.

"Can you work me in, Brother Cleo?" he asked, immediately after shaking Cleo's hand.

"Yes, sir. I only got two ahead of ya. I can work right after them."

Pastor Willis plopped down in the chair beside Coach Parker. Twenty minutes later, Cleo motioned with his index finger for him to come over and take a seat in his chair.

With a smirk on his face T-Bone began cross-examination. "Hey pastor you know a lot about the Bible so can I ask this question."

"Go ahead son."

"Well don't the Good Book says that we need to remove all sin from our lives. To get rid of the very presence of evil. Is that right pastor?"

"That right young man."

"We need to start by tearing down that sinful One Hour or Less Motel down the street. Ain't that right Pastor Willis?" he asked as he grinned.

"Now, now brother. Lets's not loose our wits about that motel."

T-Bone turned to the other men to give the men an "I told you so" with a wink.

"Let me explain something to you son, that place has opened their doors to me and the ministry. I hold a service there in the restaurant twice a week. Many people have been saved at that motel. We average about twenty salvations per week. My wife goes there early to minister to many women who are experiencing trouble at home. Later Sister Thomas and I go later and feed them. My wife and I leave satisfied that we have served the Lord."

After the pastor finished talking all the men looked over at T-Bone. He was speechless and had a sheepish look on his face. His shoulders sagged slightly knowing in his heart that he has falsely accursed Pastor Willis.

"Well," said Pastor Willis as he reached in his pocket and pulled out ten dollars plus a tip and handed it to Cleo. "You fellows have a blessed day."

After he left Coach Parker broke the silence by saying, "I heard that Pastor Cornbread is building a new church."

"Yeah," T-Bone said, "That means that he will try to raise as much money any way he possibly can to complete that building. All I know is when most churches start a building program no animal is safe. They have so many fried chicken and barbeque dinner sales that they worn me out on meat. I don't care if I see another chicken, fish, or piece of beef again," said T-Bone. "The church has almost made me a vegetarian."

Cleo simply looked at him in amazement. "See there you go again. Not all churches are like that."

"Well, if it's not food, they're having a bunch of programs."

"T-Bone you just don't understand. The truth of the matter is that if people would just pay their tithes and offerings, the church would not resort to programs. One day you will understand that the truth always comes out," he said as he picked up the basket of wet towels, put them in the washing machine, poured in some washing powder, and turned it on. "Like I always say it'll all come out in the wash."

Chapter Six
A Man That Finds a Wife Finds a Good Thing

Riley and Isaac got into his car and headed for home. Isaac looked over at him and said, "Riley, Bennie Mae's wedding made me realize something."

"What's that?" asked Riley as he stuck his arm out of the window to signal a right-hand turn.

"Georgia would make a great wife."

Riley stepped on the brake, coming to a complete halt. He scratched his head and looked over at Isaac with a puzzled look. "You mean you to tell me that you are ready to settle down? I don't believe it. What about all that noise that you would never get married in a hundred years?"

"It's hard for me to believe it too. But the fact is somehow the old girl has captured my heart. I got an idea. Let's go over to her house so I can ask her to marry me," he insisted, with an urgency in his voice.

"Don't you remember they're visiting their auntie for a few days."

"Oh, yeah. Well, let's go over there then. We both need to meet her before we marry her nieces. Do you know where she lives?"

"Yeah, Olivia gave me the directions. Here it is," he said as he took out a piece of paper from his pocket with the address on it. As he read over the paper, the people in the car behind him began to honk their horn.

"Okay, okay, keep your pants on," said Riley as he drove off. He handed the paper to Isaac.

They had driven for over an hour as Isaac carefully read off the directions. "Turn left on this street coming up," he said as he pointed.

After turning onto Clayton Street, Isaac instructed him to pull up in the second driveway on the right. They both got out of the car, walked onto the porch, and knocked on the front door. Each began to giggle knowing that the ladies would be surprised and delighted that they were there. The men heard a voice come over the loud speaker saying, "Come on in and make yourself at home."

Riley slowly opened the door as Isaac followed. They were unsure of what or who waited inside. "This is nice," said Isaac as he looked around to admire the loud purple, yellow, and orange decorations which clashed with the red carpet. "I'm going to tell Cleo that he needs to fix up the barbershop like this."

They pulled off their coats, hats, and hung them on the coat rack in the hallway before making their way into the house. The melting snow began to drip down making several small puddles on the floor. While they were talking they could feel somebody watching them.

A Man That Finds a Wife Finds a Good Thing

"Hey! We don't have any maids around here so wipe up your mess!" a mean voice yelled out.

Both men took a step backwards.

"Who said that?" Isaac whispered as he looked around to see where the voice was coming from.

An old wrinkled arm holding two white cotton bath towels appeared through the curtain that separated the hallway from the rest of the house. An old lady dressed in all white and walking with a cane suddenly appeared from behind the curtain. "I'm Sister Pauline Smith. May I help you boys?"

"Yes ma'am. We are here to see Ms. Olivia and Ms. Georgia," said Isaac as his voice trembled. Still shaken by their initial welcome.

Holding her hand to her ear she signed, "Speak up son I'm a little hard of hearing."

"We are here to see Olivia and Georgia!"

"What for?"

They took hold of the towels and got down on their knees to soak up the melting snow from the floor. "I'm Brother Riley and this here is Brother Isaac." We came to ask you to get married!"

"You came to ask me to marry ya? I keep telling everybody that if I was patient, a man would find me. Well look at this, I've hit the jackpot. I say I've hit the mother lode. Now I have two men to choose from."

The men looked at each other and shook their heads. "Oh, no ma'am you got it all wrong. We came to ask for your blessings because we want to marry your nieces!"

Disappointed by Riley's words, she responded, "Well, why didn't you speak up earlier. Follow me." The men got up off their knees and followed cautiously.

As she extended her hand, she opened the curtain and invited them into the living room. "Come on in and warm yourselves by the fire. I just made a fresh pot of coffee. Do ya'll want some?"

"Yes ma'am. We sure could use something to warm us up."

"What did you say?" as she put her hand up to her right ear again.

"Yes ma'am!" yelled Riley.

"You boys make yourselves at home. I'll be back in a few minutes."

After she left Riley said jokely, "She would make a good wife for you if Georgia turns you down." They both giggled and rushed over to the fireplace and began rubbing their hands together to warm themselves.

Isaac smiled. "I can't stand a bossy woman. But in her case I would make an exception."

Riley covered up his mouth with his hand while he giggled again. "Where do you want to sit?" As he looked around the room, he noticed that all the Victorian-style furniture was covered with plastic cleaner bags. Even the lamp shades were covered with them.

Riley suggested, "I guess we can sit anywhere we want to. We can't damage anything with all this plastic everywhere. He spotted some seats in front of the television. "Let's sit over there." He waved his arm giving him the okay to follow.

The men made their way to the two overstuffed chairs and took a seat. "Let's see if the game is on. The Cowboys are playing the Washington Red Skins in the playoffs today," said Isaac. He reached for the knob and flipped it on. He turn the channel until he finally located the game. "Man, I tell you one thing Dallas is going to skin 'em today."

"You don't know what you're talking about Isaac. The Red Skins are second in their division. They know how to play some ball." The men leaned forward as the Dallas Cowboys lost the coin toss and had to kick off the ball to the Red Skins.

Isaac pulled out a piece of aluminum foil from his coat pocket and opened it up. Inside was two pickled pig feet. "Sssh," said Riley. "Stop all that racket. I can't hear the game. "

"I'm hungry. Nothing wrong with a little snack while we watch the game is there?" he asked as he took one from the foil paper. "That Aunt Pauline is a nice lady. I'm going to ask her to make us some popcorn when she gets back." He smiled and returned to watching the game.

"What kind of mess is that!" yelled Aunt Pauline as she walked into the room holding a beautiful silver tray with a pot of coffee, cups, a sugar bowl, a cup of cream, and spoons.

"What's up her crawl?" whispered Isaac out of the side of his mouth as he was still sucking on the bones and licking his fingers.

"I don't know but her face looks like she's about to explode," Riley whispered back.

"Just wait one cotton-picking minute," she said as she placed the tray on the coffee table and walked over closer to them using her cane to help her balance. "Get up! I said get up from there and cut off my TV!" She was shaking as she walked towards them. "Everybody knows that this house is sanctified."

Completely shocked by her reaction, Isaac asked, "What's wrong with a little football?"

"Let's get one thing straight right now young man. If you're going to be a part of this family, we only watch Christian shows in this house you heathen!" She walked around him sniffing her nose for closer inspection. "I smelled sin all over ya when you first came in." While she continued talking, the noxious smell of snuff on her breath was overwhelming. Her teeth were completely stained brown from years of dipping snuff. As she talked, she spit some of the juice on Isaac's new long-sleeved white shirt. "When was the last time you been to a church you heathen? Now, tell the truth and shame the devil."

"We go to church every Sunday."

"Huh," she said as she looked up to the ceiling. "I hope a bolt of lightening don't come down from heaven and strike you dead for not telling the truth."

Isaac was quick to respond as he eyed his adversary. "I got a question for you sister. When was the last time brushed your teeth and used some mouthwash? Now tell the truth snaggle-tooth."

"What!" yelled Aunt Pauline as her eyes bulged out. She jumped back quickly putting up her fist to defend her honor. "Boy, don't be ignorant," she warned him as she stared him in the eyes and pounced around.

"Don't call me ignorant!"

"I said you're i, g, n, o, r, a, n, t," she continued as she spelled out the letters and wrote each letter in the air.

"I told you not to call me ignorant," demanded Isaac.

"I'm sorry. You're right, you're not ignorant. But your mama's ignorant, your daddy's ignorant, even your dog's ignorant!"

"Now look you can talk about my daddy and you can talk about me. But nobody, I mean nobody talks about my mama or my dog. You're going down old lady!"

"Isaac and Ms. Pauline!" said Riley as he tried to separate the two. "Let's all calm down seeing that we'll all going to be family and all."

"Young man, no way I'm going to let this ignorant heathen into my family. All I can say is your friend better be glad you came with him because I was about to lay down my religion and let him have it." Aunt Pauline balled up her fist again and began jabbing the air like a boxer.

"Get back old lady before I deck ya," said Isaac as he raised his fist.

"Son, you don't know me but I'll take your head clean off." Aunt Pauline took her cane from under her arm, twirled it around her hand like a skilled combat fighter, and grabbed him by the neck. "Tell sweet Jesus hello cause you are about to meet your maker boy." Then with a quick kick to his knees, she yanked him to the floor. "Well, go ahead with your bad self," she said as she placed one foot on his chest like David about to slay the giant.

Then Riley started laughing at Isaac as Aunt Pauline pulled the cane tighter around his neck.

"Anybody else want to challenge me?"

"No ma'am. Your 'da man," proclaimed Riley. "I was taught to respect my elders. Please don't hold it against that heathen ma'am." He was chuckling under his breath.

She abruptly removed the wooden cane from around Isaac's neck, graciously stuck it out, and gently touched Riley on the head to pardon him like a queen with her scepter.

"Aunt Pauline, what are you doing?" asked Georgia as she walked into the room. "Let him up before you hurt him. I told you about that. Sorry about that Isaac.

Sometimes my aunt can be mean as two Doberman pinchers."

Riley held out a hand and helped Isaac up off the floor. Isaac swallowed and rubbed his neck. "If you had not come out when you did, I would have hurt your auntie," Isaac confessed as he dusted himself off.

"Is that so? Well, we can take this outside if you like," urged Aunt Pauline. "And you want to marry my niece! No way Jose."

"Hush, Aunt Pauline and let the man speak," Georgia's eyes widened with excitement as she compelled her to be quiet.

"Well, I came over here to ask you to marry me but . . ."

"I don't want you to marry him," she ordered. "He's a heathen. I wouldn't spit on him if he was on fire," said Aunt Pauline as she shook her finger at him.

"You did spit on me already old lady," Isaac replied as he pointed to his speckled white shirt. "But every dog has his day."

Before she could answer, he stepped behind Riley for protection. "Aunt Pauline he's not a heathen. Now you go to your room and I will come in later and bring you a nice cup of hot chocolate."

"Okay," she said as she kissed Georgia on the cheek and walked towards her room. "I want marshmallows in it this time." She stuck her neck out and hissed as she passed Isaac.

After Aunt Pauline left the room, Isaac got down on one knee, and cleared his throat. Then he grabbed Georgia by the hand and asked, "Georgia, will you marry me?"

"Of course, I will Mr. Isaac. I mean Isaac. I would be honored to have you as my husband. When?" she asked as she look down at him.

"I don't want to waste any money . . . I mean time. We can get married when Riley and Olivia get married." He stood up and looked over at Riley. "We can have a double-wedding ceremony."

"You and Riley can move in with us. We have two bedrooms you know."

Olivia walked out just in time to hear Isaac propose. "Yeah, you and Riley can have one of the rooms and Georgia and I can sleep in the other."

"Now let's settle one thing right now," said Riley. "Nobody's sleeping in the bed with my honey but me once we're married."

"And the same goes for me," said Isaac.

"Well, okay but I don't see what difference it makes," said Olivia.

"It does make a difference," said Riley as he looked over at Isaac and smiled. "No offense, Isaac, but I don't want to snuggle up to you on a cold winter night."

"Georgia, I'm sorry but I didn't have time to look for an engagement ring. It all happened so fast." Then he remembered something. He pulled out a piece of the aluminum foil from his pocket. Made it into a ring and placed it on her finger. "When we get back we're going shopping for the ring you like."

Moved, Riley reached to take Olivia's hand also. "I going to buy my sweet Olivia the biggest wedding ring I can find." Each man was true to his word because they both had found a good thing.

Wake Up & Smell the Coffee!

Chapter Seven
If the Shoe Fits, Wear It

One Week Later

"Hurry up Olivia or we're gonna be late," said Georgia as she looked in the mirror to put on her false eyelashes.

"Okay, okay! But don't rush me. You know how that makes me nervous. You know it takes extra time to put on these support hose," she said as she struggled to pull them up. As she was speaking and not paying attention to what she was doing, one of her fingernails accidently caught her pantyhose and ripped them.

"Oooh! Look what you made me do!"

"Don't try to blame that on me. If you started getting ready earlier, you wouldn't have to rush."

"Stop complaining and tell me what time we're supposed to be at the church."

"Eight o'clock," said Georgia as she looked at her watch.

Olivia asked, "Do know where my black shoes are?"

"You're always looking for stuff. If you put your stuff where it belongs, you would find it when you needed it."

"Who me?"

"Yes you. Like mama used to say, 'If the shoe fits wear it!'"

"I can't find my stuff because you always claim that it's yours. Take off one of those shoes and let me see if my name is written inside of it."

Georgia looked into Olivia's brown eyes. "I will not! These are not your shoes, they're mine. You know good and well that I could not fit into those narrow shoes of yours."

"Oh yeah! I forget that you have plump feet. Why, your feet would hang over the sides. Just like they are doing now if they were mine."

"My feet are not hanging over the sides of my shoes. That's the way they are suppose to fit. And I've told you before that I don't like nobody talking about my feet."

"Did I say feet. What I meant to say was those boats!"

Georgia closed her eyes for a second, making a visible effort to stay calm. "Boats! Oooh, you are impossible!" She threw both of her hands in the air.

"Yeah, boats. Your feet are so big it look like you are walking on jet skies."

As the conversation was heating up they heard a horn blowing outside. Georgia sat down on the bed and peeped out of the curtains. "I think it's Brother Riley but he's driving a different car. Take a look."

"It is Riley," said Olivia as she opened the curtain wider to look out. "What kind of junk is he driving?

"I'm sure that it looks better on the inside," Georgia said as she turned to continue primping in the mirror. "I'm glad that Brother Riley likes to be on time unlike certain other folks that I know. That's why I told you to hurry up."

"It only takes ten minutes to get to the church. It's only seven-thirty. I told him not to be here until seven forty-five. That man never listens to a word that I tell him. He'll just have to wait until I'm finished."

Georgia made her way to the living room mumbling all the way under her breath. "You're never ready on time. You're gonna be late to your own funeral if the Lord tarries."

Riley was driving and Isaac was riding shotgun on the passenger side. Riley rolled down the window, stuck his head outside, and blew his horn to proclaim the wonderful news of their arrival. He cut the engine and looked over at Isaac. "I hope they're ready," he said as the frost could be seen coming from his mouth as he talked.

Olivia took her blue shoes out of the closet, sat them down the floor, slipped them on, and headed for the living room. By then, Georgia was brewing up a good temper. Olivia looked at Georgia's face. She was fuming.

"Are you ready now!" asked Georgia.

"You got eyes. See for yourself." Olivia grabbed her gloves and long handled black umbrella off the small coffee table in the living room. "Let's go before you make me so mad that I'll say something I'll regret." After they both had put on their coats and scarves, they slowly made their way out through the front door and towards the car.

Riley was the first to spot them coming. "Here they come." He looked over at Isaac and said, "Olivia's a looker ain't she. I can't wait for us to get married. I can't help but think about that girl must be a love machine."

Both men got out of the car and waited for the ladies to make their way down the sidewalk. "I don't know any sisters that get along so well as those two."

"Me either," said Isaac as the women approached the car.

"Riley, didn't I tell you to be here at seven forty-five?"

Riley took Olivia by her arm and escorted her around to the passenger side and opened the door for her. "Now, honey bunch, I know you said to be here at that time but I couldn't wait to see you." Riley shut the door behind her and ran back around to the driver's side, opened his door and got inside.

Isaac opened Georgia's door and hopped in behind her. "Georgia you look plum beautiful."

"Thank you," she said as she blushed.

"What time do we have to be at the church?"

"We are meeting the Board of Elders at eight o'clock," said Olivia. "So step on it!"

The women were not very enthusiastic about meeting with the Board. They knew first hand that the board was not a push over. They were a very hard group to pass inspection. The men on the other hand could not wait. They knew that they would receive the seal of approval with flying colors.

As the car pulled out of the driveway, one of the hub cabs broke free and flew across the road before coming to rest on the curb. Huge billows of black smoke rose out of the tail pipe as the car backfired several times.

Olivia could not resist the opportunity to make a comment. "This don't make no sense. You need to do something about this car before somebody gets hurt. Sounds like we are in a war zone. Why did you drive this piece of junk instead of the Cadillac?" Olivia wrinkled her forehead.

Riley laughed, flexed his fingers on the steering wheel, and focused on his driving.

She spoke again. "I asked you a question. Why did you drive this piece of junk over here?"

"All Betsy needs is a little paint and a tune up. The old girl will be as good as new. They don't make cars like this anymore. I plan on keeping her another twenty if the good Lord says so. She has gotten me through three wars and she be with me till Jesus comes.

She's solid as a rock." As he pounded on the dash board several times to prove his point, the radio lost its hold and fell out into Olivia's lap.

"Yeah you're right. They don't make 'em like this any more." She could feel the springs from the seat poking her in her back. Olivia reached over and turned on what she though was the heater. Gray smoke poured in through the vents. As she waved the smoke from her face, she said, "It's cold in here. Don't tell me you don't have any heat."

"Sho' do." He hit the dash five times and flipped on a knob. Warm air began to circulate in the car. "You'll learn how to work Old Betsy in no time." He put his arm across the back of her seat. "Feeling better?"

"Don't try no funny stuff with me!" exclaimed Olivia as she hit Riley across the knee cap with her umbrella. "Does that feel better," she said as she grinned. He rubbed his knee with one hand and drove with the other.

"By the way, what speed are we going?" asked Olivia as she glanced over at the speedometer. The needle was moving rapidly back and forth from thirty-five to sixty-five miles per hour.

"Don't know, it's broke."

"How do you know what speed you are going then?"

"It's easy, I just go with the flow of the traffic."

"When did you get this car?"

"I've had it for years but I only use it for special occasions. I'm planning to drive her to our honeymoon hideaway. I was thinking about painting a sign on her for our wedding day and change to old girl name from Betsy to the Love Mobile." The car made a few backfiring noises.

Olivia gave him a funny look. "I'm not even going to respond to that. Brother Riley, do you remember where the church is at?" She looked at him through the rear view mirror.

"What you asking him for?" asked Riley in a jealous tone. He don't even know how to get across the street." He stuck his arm out the window to signal a right hand turn. Isaac was laughing so hard that his side began to hurt.

"All I have to do is just make a right turn onto Winchester Road and a left turn on Parks Avenue. At this next stop sign, that's Winchester Road."

As he approached a stop sign, he did not stop but keep straight on through.

"What's wrong with you Riley? Didn't you see that stop sign?" said Olivia angrily.

"Well, I guess I didn't pump my brakes long enough."

"What?" exclaimed Olivia in a loud tone. "You mean to tell me you don't have any brakes?"

"Yeah, if I pump 'em I do."

"You have got to be kidding me." Olivia looked down from the speedometer to the floorboard as she clenched the seat. She stared at him. "Help us dear Jesus to get there in one piece and on time," was all she kept murmuring the rest of the way to the church.

Riley was in no hurry to get there. His mind was not on what time they had to be there, what speed they were traveling or the brakes. Nor was he thinking about the convenience store, mobile home park, or downtown that slid past. All he could think about was Olivia.

As Riley pulled up in front of Abundant Love Church, he could see that a fresh blanket of snow had covered the roof top and smoke rising up from the chimney.

The church was a small, old, white wood-framed building but it welcomed many that was graced to step through its doors.

Isaac slid over to the other side of the car, and squeezed closer to Georgia. Reaching over, he rolled down the back window, and stuck out his head. "Who is that going in the church? They look like a pack of angry buffalos."

Georgia reached in her purse, pulled out her glasses, and put them on. "That's the Board of Elders we told you about."

Isaac stuck his head out the window to get a better view. "The way they look there might not be a wedding."

"Nobody, I mean nobody is going to stop me from marrying the woman that I love," Riley stated boldly.

Olivia smiled at such a forceful response. "I love a man that takes authority. Now hurry up and let me out of this piece of junk. You got me," she said sternly.

"Yes, puddin."

Riley jumped out of the car and ran around to the other side of the car to open the door for Olivia and Georgia.

"When I get home, I want you to bury this piece of junk."

"Yes, puddin," he said as he nodded his head and opened the back door to the church.

As they approached counciling office, Olivia gave a quiet knock on the door. Then, she opened it. Mother Hennetta Seal, Mother Faye Jackson, and Mother Erma Jones sat at a large conference table and remained absolutely poker-faced as the couples stepped inside. The elders were ready to grill, roast, and if necessary toast them.

After Mother Seal spotted Olivia and Georgia she asked, "Well, what are you all doing here?"

"We are the newlyweds to be," Georgia proudly admitted.

"Can't be," commented Mother Seal.

"Surely not. Aren't you'll a little old to be getting married?" asked Mother Jackson.

"Yes, too old if you ask me," said Mother Jones.

"I can't believe they said that," whispered Olivia to Georgia.

"Why, that was so rude," Georgia whispered back.

"Now listen here you old bats," Isaac responded.

"Quiet, all of you," said Mother Seal as she struck the table with her gavel. "Now as you all know, it is up to us to determine who should be married in this church. We are responsible for examining the bride and groom's character to see if they are ready for marriage. We are the only ones, I mean the only ones that can pass a recommendation on to the Pastor. So if I were you, I would treat us with the utmost respect. Now apologize or you will be sorry."

"Please apologize, Isaac," requested Riley.

"I apologize that you're old bats."

"Okay I accept . . . I think," Mother Jones said with a uncertain look on her face.

"Well, have a seat, you are holding us up," demanded Mother Seal.

The couples scrambled for a seat.

"Any objections?" said Mother Seal. Silence fell in the room. "I said is there, any objections!" She frowned and looked around the table.

"No," everyone responded in unison.

"Fine! We shall proceed. We will first examine any discrepancies on your applications. She looked over the applications and asked, "Why didn't you two ladies list your ages? It's things like this that slows down the application process."

"Does it matter?" asked Georgia. "We are over twenty-one."

"That is quite obvious by your appearance," Mother Seal said sarcastically as she leaned over, pulled her glasses to the tip of her nose, and bucked her eyes. We can tell you two are no spring chickens. Now what are your ages?"

"We are both seventy-five years."

"I didn't know you were that old Georgia," noted Isaac.

"Anybody your age really should devote the rest of their lives to serving the Lord like us. It gives us great joy to do what we are doing," she said as she frowned.

"Yes, you should only be thinking of God at your age. The Lord is our husband," said Mother Jackson.

Isaac leaned over and whispered in Riley's ear, "If the old broads had a man in their life they wouldn't look like wrinkled old prunes." Riley snickered quietly.

"Are you ready to proceed with the next phase of questioning?" asked Mother Seal. Everyone nodded.

"What will you be wearing?"

"We both will wear a full length white wedding dress of course, with a bouquet of white lilies," said Olivia.

"Yes, with a full train," continued Georgia.

"Hold up a minute," said Mother Jackson. "There is a question we have to ask before we proceed."

"Yeah," said Mother Jones. "First we have to know if you have ever . . ."

"Ever what?"

"You know ever . . ." she said as she lifted up an eyebrow. "You know . . . Brother Riley or Brother Isaac ever been in either of ya'lls cedar chest?"

"What!" yelled Olivia in a state of shock as her mouth dropped wide open. "No! What type of women do you think we are?" asked Olivia. "I've never even kissed a man before."

Angry by even the thought of the question, Georgia hastily stood up in protest. She placed both of her hands on the table and leaned over towards the Elders. "Olivia has never been spoiled by no man and neither have I! Like my mama always said, 'You can't have the milk unless you buy the cow,'" stated Georgia as Olivia nodded her head in total agreement.

The Board smiled at the response. "That is almost unheard of these days," said Mother Seal.

"Yes, almost unheard of," said Mother Jones.

"Mothers," said Riley, "I've always been a gentleman when I'm around Olivia. But I have one question."

"What is it, Brother Riley?" asked Mother Jackson.

"Well, is there anything wrong with a little smooching before we get married?"

Olivia was quite embarrassed by the question. "Hush, Riley," urged Olivia as she patted him on the hand. "I don't want everybody to know our business."

"What business? I can't hug ya, I can't kiss ya, I can't hold your hand. You won't budge. So I want an answer from these wise women of God as to why I can't at least get a smooch from you once in a while."

"Well, Brother Riley," said Mother Nelson after clearing her throat. "The Good Book says to abstain from even the appearance of evil. Don't you agree Mother Jackson?"

"Oh yes. I believe it's best that smooching wait until after the wedding," said Mother Jackson.

"Yes, there is plenty of time for that stuff afterwards. It can lead to more serious things," said Mother Seal. "What do you think Mother Jones?"

"Yes, more serious things," commented Mother Jones

"Smooching?" questioned Riley.

"Yes, smooching. It causes the body to act ungodly."

"Ungodly?" questioned Riley again.

"Yes, ungodly," continued Mother Jones, "Then it's too late to shut the gate once the cows have gotten out."

"What's ungodly about a man wanting to show his woman that he loves her? That don't make no sense to me."

"Brother Riley let me break it down to ya. Don't you realized that your hormones could go berserk and the next thing you know, nine months later, Sister Olivia could be walking around with a little surprise package weighing seven pounds and eight ounces."

"Hush, Riley," Olivia demanded more firmly.

"Now darling, I've got a right to ask questions don't I?"

"Yeah, let him speak his mind for a change," insisted Georgia.

"Georgia, you stay out if this," commanded Olivia.

Georgia looked over at Olivia. "I know what you're talking about because she's as stubborn as a mule and bossy. Ain't she, Brother Riley?"

"Well, sometimes she can be a little bossy," Riley added, "But I don't mind."

"Bossy! Why Riley, I can't believe you said that," Olivia expressed in an unbelieving tone.

"Well, honey sometimes you are too bossy," Riley said.

"Well, what about you? You're so jealous that you're always smothering me."

"She got you there, Riley. You are too jealous," said Isaac.

"Isaac, you argue about everything," continued Olivia.

"Wait, Olivia! Don't talk about my beloved like that," Georgia interjected.

"You're the one that told me that, Georgia. See, Georgia, your problem is you can't hold water," said Olivia.

"Georgia, you told her that I like to argue?" questioned Isaac.

"Well, I didn't quite mean it like that."

"Well, what did you mean?"

"I meant that you have a strong opinion about everything."

"Oh, that's better," said Isaac. "I thought that you were talking about me behind my back."

"Order! Order!" demanded Mother Nelson as she struck her gavel on the table. "Apparently you all don't understand something. I can't believe you want to get married with all this sinful behavior that is not pleasing to God. First of all, Olivia, you can't boss people around. That's wrong and God ain't please with that. You can't boss people around like an animal. You are suppose to love them."

Mother Nelson continued. "Brother Riley, jealousy is sin. If God gave her to ya, nobody can take her away."

"You're right but I got a right to protect her. That's what men are for. That's what my daddy always told me."

"That's ungodly council, Brother Riley."

"Yeah, Riley, ungodly council," said Olivia.

"Now listen, you can't be with Sister Olivia all the time. You have to trust the Lord to take care of her. That's the Lord's job. Some things we learn are wrong. It is up to us to get into God's word and find out the truth. As for you, Sister Georgia, you shouldn't gossip about people. You have to learn to guard your mouth."

"Well, if people don't appreciate me trying to give them news to help them, I sure will keep my mouth shut. I'll just zip my lip and throw away the key." Then she acted it out.

"The Bible says that gossip is like dainty morsels and you sow discord," added Mother Jackson.

"Yeah, Georgia, dainty morsels," said Olivia.

"Brother Isaac, you can't be right all the time. If you spend as much time in the Word of God as you do trying to prove that you're right you would a powerful man of God.

"I know I need to work on it."

The Elders huddled together to compare notes. After deliberating for only five minutes, Mother Seal said, "Ya'll act like ya'll are married already. So it is the decision of this committee that the union for the both of ya'll may proceed."

Mother Nelson took out the official elder seal. She opened the black ink to wet it and stamped the official documents approving the wedding.

"Thank you," said Riley as he grabbed each of their hands.

"Yes, thank all of you," said Olivia, Georgia, and Isaac. The couples made their way out of the office rejoicing.

Mother Seals turned to the rest of the mothers. "I'll give 'em three good years and they will be sorry they ever knew each other."

Chapter Eight
Wake Up and Smell the Coffee!

The Wedding Day

Single women from every surrounding town had gotten wind of the wedding and made plans to attend. Each woman was determined to take down every single man in the place. Plots were formed and battle plans were drawn. The fighting would be fierce and the casualties would be many. Every bachelor would be taken "Dead or Alive." Not one would escape.

The church parking lot was almost full by the time Lulu and Francis drove up. The feeling of anticipation heightened within them as they made their way up out of the car and up the wooden steps of the church to open the door.

An usher named Richard Robertson greeted them with a handshake as they stepped inside.

"Hello," Lulu said in a very flirtatious manner.

"I'm married already," he stated up front as he displayed his wedding band. "Well, I just wanted to let you ladies know up front. I've had at least fifty marriage proposals since I've been here."

Francis rolled her eyes. "Who cares."

"Yeah, who cares. You're not our type any way," Lulu said as she flung her hand out.

Richard could not wait to see their faces as he opened the doors that lead into the sanctuary. "Well, I hope you ladies brought seats," he stated jokingly.

The ladies were puzzled by his comment and did not know exactly how to respond to it. Inside was a scene beyond anything they had expected. Francis was in amazement as she turned her head from side to side. Rows of family, friends, and desperate single women had gathered there, waiting for the wedding to begin.

"Girl, look at all these women. I wonder where they all came from?"

Disappointed by the shortage of seats and abundance of women, Lulu's voice reflected her thoughts. "I don't know. Now you see what I was talking about. That's why I told you that we needed to leave earlier. I wanted us to be the first ones here so we could get a good seat." They began hunting for a place to sit like vultures looking for prey.

"There's two over there," said Francis as she pointed across the room. "Come on if we hurry we can get over there before somebody beats us to 'em."

"There must be hundreds of desperate single women here," remarked Lulu as she walked quickly with Francis right on her heels. Before they took their seats they glanced around the room in disbelief. "Look over there," she said as nudged her head to the left.

"There's Misty Brown. That woman would do anything to get a husband. And look over there," she gently nudged her head to the right. "Isn't that Leslie Campbell and Peaches Norwood?" she asked as she pointed her eyes in their direction.

"Now there's two desperate women if I ever saw any," Francis added. "Even the Calhoun sisters are here, Pearl Ann, Jenny Mae, Susie Lou, Jackie Faye, Julie Ray, and Little Biscuit. They know they don't stand a chance of finding a man. I don't know why they even bothered to show up. No man in his right mind would marry a Calhoun. Wait a minute, girl," she said as she grabbed Lulu by the arm. "I don't believe it. Isn't that Old Lady Andrews?" Francis and Lulu shared a look.

"Yeah, it's her alright," Lulu said. "That's pitiful ain't it. She told me she was going to be here looking for a husband. I didn't believe her but the woman was telling the truth."

"She can barely walk."

"That goes to show you that age doesn't matter when a woman wants a man. You know, she almost died at least five or six times."

After they had taken their seats Francis remarked, "Yeah, girl, I heard. That woman's like a cat with nine lives. You know that the last time we were here for a wedding they threw us out. Remember?"

"I know, but this time it's going to be different," Lulu boldly stated as she aimed her finger at Francis. I'm not leaving without me a husband-to-be. And I tell you another thing." She paused to take a short breath. "I ain't playing when I say that these women better stay out of my way today. I'm not allowing another woman to take a man from me. Never again." A tear rolled down her cheek as she thought of Bennie Mae.

"Yeah," replied Francis. As she began to rub Lulu on her back. "Look at all these men, girl. Surely there's got to be at least a couple of good ones in the bunch for us," she said trying to cheer up Lulu.

While Francis looked around the room she noticed that Reverend and Sister Pearle were sitting on the other side of the church. "Look over there."

"Look at what?"

"Don't you see 'em."

"See who?"

"There's Reverend Pearle and his hopefully soon to be ex-wife," Francis said, keeping her eyes on the both of them. She hunched Lulu in the side with her elbow. "What she's got that I haven't got?"

"She's got the Reverend." Lulu then took out a handkerchief and blew her nose.

A few rows ahead of them was the gang from the barbershop. "Isn't that T-Bone?" Francis asked as she lifted herself up off the pew.

"Yeah, it sure is. I didn't know he was going to be here. This is a blessing." She took out a pen and a piece of paper and wrote T-Bone's name on the top of her list.

"Winford!" she yelled out as she waved to him. "You hoo, Winford!"

T-Bone turned around to see who was calling his name. "Oh, no. It's Lulu. She's just as country as she wants to be." Embarrassed by the unwanted attention, he slid down in his seat.

She turned to Francis and told her, "He's trying to play hard to get. But he might as well understand that he is mine."

"Winford? Man, I didn't know your name was Winford," Coach Parker teased. "What kind of name is that?"

T-Bone left eyebrow rose sharply. "For your information it's a high class name. But only people with class would understand. So that means you're out of the picture."

"I have plenty of class," replied Coach Parker as he belched.

"You're like that boy that went to school on Saturday, no class."

Before Coach Parker could respond he began to sniff the air. "I smell popcorn."

"That's your imagination," T-Bone insisted. "No one serves popcorn at a wedding. See that's what I mean, no class. That's probably some fancy gourmet dish they are cooking to take to the reception."

"Well, I guess you're right. But it sure smells like popcorn." While he was sampling the air, in walked Pastor Cornbread with a strap around his neck that held a tray out in front of him.

"Popcorn, popcorn!" he yelled out. "Get your popcorn."

"See, I told you I smelled popcorn," said Coach Parker with confidence as he hunched T-Bone.

"What in the world is he doing?" asked T-Bone. "Who would sell popcorn at a wedding?"

"A man trying to build a church," said Coach Parker. "Sounds like a good idea to me. I think I'm going to buy a bag. I didn't have any dinner this evening. Hey, Pastor over here." He bid him to come over with the wave of his hand.

"How is the church project coming, Pastor?" asked T-Bone. "Ya'll have been raising money for that building fund for a long time. But I don't see nothing happening."

"Well, all I can say is that the Lord has been mighty good to the church. All we need is about three-thousand dollars, then we can start pouring the foundation. Have you fellows made a donation yet?"

"Well," said T-Bone. "If I could get more paying customers, I could help you Pastor." Right now I'm just trying to keep my lights on and a shirt on my back."

"What about you, Coach Parker?"

"Pastor, I already have several times already," answered Coach Parker.

"Oh, but it's not too late if you want to make another contribution. Remember, it's more blessed to give then to receive."

"Okay how much for the popcorn?" Coach Parker asked as he took out a dollar.

"That will be five dollars."

"Five dollars? That's highway robbery."

"Well, if you don't want it I have plenty of customers waiting. About that time other people began to wave and signal the pastor to come their way."

"Okay," he said reluctantly as he reached in his pocket and took out four more dollars and handed them to him.

"Thanks and you get one refill with that Brother Parker." Then, he headed for his next customer.

"Now there's a man that knows how to raise a dollar," said Coach Parker as he crammed popcorn into his mouth. T-Bone started laughing.

"Hey, T-Bone, where's Cleo?"

"He'll be here. He putting the finishing touches on the reception he's throwing at the barbershop after we leave here."

"I wonder why nobody told me."

"Now Coach, you know your wife is not going to let you be out that late."

"Let's get one thing straight. My wife don't run me. I'm my own man. I can stay out as late as I want to. Even all night if I want to." About that time his cellular telephone rang.

"I didn't know you had a cell phone."

"Yeah, my wife just bought it for me." The cellular telephone kept ringing for the sixth time.

"You better get that man. It might be her calling." T-Bone smiled.

"Hello," said Coach Parker as he tried to whisper. He thought to himself, *for once I wish that she would leave me alone.* "I know it took me a while to answer. I'm at the wedding. I can't talk louder. I said I'm at the wedding. Honey, can I go to the reception after the wedding? What do you mean no," as his voice got louder. Like a child whining he continued, "You never let me have any fun." Apologetically he said, "No, I don't want to sleep on the couch. Okay dear. Yes dear, I will come home as soon as the wedding is over. Goodbye." He turned to T-Bone with a sheepish look. "Huh, I told her a thing or two," he confirmed as he nodded his head.

As he was slipping the cellular telephone into its holder on his belt, Cleo snuck in quietly and took a seat beside T-Bone. He whispered. "Hey did I miss anything?"

"Naw. They haven't even started the show yet. Is everything set for the reception?"

"Man we're going to party down tonight. You remember that Christian band I was telling you about, Creole Mix?"

"Uh-huh."

"Well they are going to be there."

"Man they're good."

"And we have so much food that we could feed an army." As he was talking, in walked Barbara Ann Smith. Immediately Cleo's mouth dropped open as he stared at her. He was breathless. She was the most beautiful woman he had ever seen.

"Cleo, Cleo," said T-Bone as he shook his arm. "Cleo snap out of it man."

Cleo could not take his eyes off of her. He turned his head to follow her as she walked up the aisle and took a seat on the second row.

Barbara Ann was strikingly beautiful. She was a green-eyed, slender built Creole beauty. She stood about six feet tall and weighed one hundred forty-five pounds. She wore her shoulder length black hair in a french twist with Shirley Temple curls down the sides of her face. Her olive complexion complimented the eloquent white suit with pink sequined roses on the front, white beaded shoes, and a white beaded evening bag under her arm. As she moved towards them with measured grace, Cleo could smell the fresh peach scent perfume that she wore.

"Who is that?" he asked as he moved his head from side to side, to get a peak at her through the crowd.

"I don't know man but I can tell you this, she's a twenty on a ten point scale," said T-Bone. "That's the kind of woman a man can fall in love with quick. I'm staying away from her as far as I can."

"That's her."

"Her who?"

"The woman I'm going to marry," said Cleo as he released a sigh of relief.

"Get out of here, Cleo. You don't even know her."

"That's going to change as soon as this wedding is over."

Sister Beluah, began to play soft wedding melodies on the organ. Pastor Cornbread rushed to the back to his office to change his clothes. All heads turned towards the rear of the church as Aunt Pauline proudly strolled down the aisle with her wooden cane in her hand and a brother on each arm. Uncle Joedale on one arm, and Uncle Bunt on the other.

Aunt Pauline whispered in Uncle Bunt's ear, "Bunt if you or Joedale mess up this wedding in any way I'm going to hurt you'll bad." He knew that she meant exactly what she said.

"Now, Pauline, you know I wouldn't do anything to mess up my nieces' wedding day. Jokingly he commented, "It took us too long to get rid of them." He looked over at her and assured her with a smile. It was obvious that she did not appreciate the remark by the frown on her face. "I'm sorry," Uncle Bunt continued, in the same joking tone. "I'll try to behave myself. I'm going to check on the girls. I'll be back before the wedding starts."

As both brides were putting on their make-up neither had spoken a word to each other all day. Uncle Bunt knocked on the door.

"Come in," said Olivia.

"Girls, you both look beautiful. This is how your Aunt Pauline and your mother's wedding should have been."

"What do you mean Uncle?" inquired Georgia.

"Well, I know your Aunt Pauline never talked about it but she and your mama Earline were twins too."

Georgia and Olivia's mouth dropped opened.

"What?" exclaimed Georgia. "We never knew that."

"Yep, they show were. I remember when they were growing up they fought about anything and everything. They were always making a mountain out of a mole hill. I remember the time when your mama stole Pauline's boyfriend in the tenth grade. Once he met your mama he broke up with Pauline and a few years later he married her. Your aunt vowed never to speak to her again. But they made up and Pauline forgave her. But that wasn't the straw that broke the camels back."

"If that didn't do it what did?" questioned Olivia as she looked over at Georgia with a puzzled look.

"Well, it had to do with this bed that our mama bought them when they were teenagers. They were always fighting over who really owned it. One night

Earline stole the bed and hid it. So for twenty-five years the feud was on. By the time she finally decided to forgive your mother, it was too late."

"Uncle how did this bed look?" asked Georgia.

"It was some type of fancy mahogany wood bed with the initials "P" for Pauline and "E" for Earline carved in it. I'm glad she didn't pass that mess on to the two of you. I believe that since they were always arguing in it, that bed must be cursed." He took a deep breathe and smiled. "Well, I'm going out there and wrestle with Pauline for a good seat. I'm the best man you know."

They glanced at each other as their eyes told the whole story. The thought ran through both of their minds at the same time, *That's our bed.*

After he had left, Olivia turned to Georgia and said, "Mama must have chipped out the "P" for Aunt Pauline's initial. Sister, I don't want us to end up like mama and Aunt Pauline, not speaking to each other. I've been mean to you over the years haven't I?"

"Olivia, it was not all your fault. I have not been the sister you deserved either. What happened to us? We use to be close until we got grown."

"I don't know. I guess pride, jealousy, and foolishness creep in. Will you forgive me?" asked Olivia.

"Of course I will. But I'm just as guilty. I have always been jealous of the relationship you and mama had. She always seem to treat you special," said Georgia.

Olivia walked over and grabbed Georgia's hand. "I guess that you didn't know that she always admired how you could stand up to her when she was wrong. I believed she realized that you were just like her. I just want you to know that she loved you dearly."

"Really? I hope you can forgive me."

"Of course I can if you can forgive me as well. From now on, our relationship is going to be different. The first thing we must do is have the bed restored with Aunt Pauline's initial. Then give that bed to her. What do you think?"

"Yes, that's the right thing to do."

They both started crying and hugging each other when they heard a knock on the door.

"Who is it?" asked Olivia as she sniffled.

"It's me Uncle Joedale."

"Come in."

"Hey, what's going on in here? Why all the tears? This is a time to celebrate. My, my, my," he said as he looked them over. "Girls, you both look beautiful. I mean simply beautiful. Before your mama went to be with the Lord she made me promise that we would see after you both until ya'll found husbands to take care of ya. She would be so proud of how you both turned out. Now look at ya. All grown up. He took a handkerchief out of his coat pocket and blew his nose. "Now you two have started to make me cry."

Olivia and Georgia kissed him on the cheek.

"Are you ready?" he asked as he opened the door. They all took a deep breath.

"Yes, we're ready," said Georgia as she and Olivia headed for the door.

Pastor Cornbread made his entrance from his office followed by the two grooms.

"Are you fellows ready?" he asked.

Isaac nodded, ignoring the flash of unease that whipped though his stomach as he did. *Wedding jitters,* he thought. *Most grooms probably experienced them. More than likely, there was nothing to worry about,* he said to himself.

"I was born ready," Riley told him.

And he had been. He was the type of man that loved to be married. He married his first wife when he was only eighteen. Now since she was in glory, he knew he needed another good Christian woman to live out the rest of his years with. He was ready to settle down with his soul mate, Olivia Nelson.

Riley and Isaac were both grinning like Cheshire cats. Isaac let out a loud burp. Then, he burped again. Riley whispered to him, "I don't know why you ate those pig feet before we left. You know it always gives you gas." He fanned the smell away from his face.

"I had to have a snack before a wedding. They don't serve you real food at receptions," said Isaac.

"Not at our reception. We've got a feast waiting for us after the wedding. Cleo hired a band and a catering service. It's all just waiting for us at the barbershop."

"I can't wait," Isaac said as he licked his lips.

The brides appeared at the back of the church as Uncle Joedale grabbed each by the arm as they awaited their cue to walk down the aisle. The smell of moth ball lingered on their wedding dresses from being stored in the cedar chest for decades. Sister Beulah softly started playing the song "Here Comes the Bride" on the old pipe organ with all her might as she rocked from side to side. The congregation stood to their feet as they slowly walked past each row. There was a barrage of camera flashes and video camera lights.

"Look at her Isaac. My Olivia is so beautiful. I'm the most blessed man on this earth."

"Yeah and look at Georgia. She looks like a bucket of Kentucky Fried Chicken. Finger licking good," Isaac jested as they both grinned and looked at each other.

After the women made their way to the altar, Pastor Cornbread told the audience, "You may be seated. We have gathered together to join these two couples in holy matrimony. Marriage is a serious commitment between two people. Some of you are here today who are married know what I'm talking about. I can tell by the crowd that there are a lot of you singles out there looking for a mate. Now, especially to you single women, the Good Book says that a man who finds a wife finds a good thing. That means that you woman are not supposed to be looking for a mate. A good man doesn't want a woman to chase him like he's some type of rabbit or coon. Amen."

"Amen," commented some of the men in the congregation.

"I tell you something else. If you end up with the wrong man you will regret it the rest of your days. Amen."

Francis stood to her feet and waved her hand in agreement and shouted "Amen!" The rest of the congregation of brokenhearted women followed suit.

"No doubt some of you women are here today thinking you are going to go home with a husband or possibly a good lead."

"That's right," whispered Lulu to Francis.

"But you better let the Lord lead you instead of your eyes. A good man is worth the wait. Amen."

"Amen!" responded the men.

"Before I marry these couples today, I want to tell you something about being married," said Pastor Cornbread. "Remember this one thing and this will save you a lot of grief in the end. You married the whole package not just the wrapper." He bidded his wife to come forth. "You see this woman. When I married her, she had a sixties Coke bottle figure. My sweet Emma was a sight to behold in her hay day. But some how the years have taken a cruel toll on her. Along with all the pies, cakes, candy bars, steaks, rice,

128

and gravy. Now she's built like a two liter. And under that black wig of hers is hair as white as lamb wool." With his hand, he tried to lift a portion of her wig to expose what she was trying to conceal. She grabbed her wig and slapped his hand.

"And my Emma has more corns on her feet than corn on the cob," he said as he giggled and the congregation joined in. "But she's still my little butterball and I love her just as much as I did then."

T-Bone turned to Cleo and whispered, "Just think, if you do marry that girl, she will probably look like that in twenty years. Wearing false teeth, orthopedic shoes, and round like a one gallon milk jug."

"Shhh," whispered Cleo.

"Would you like to say something, mama?" he asked as he handed her the microphone.

Emma said, "The first few years of marriage were rough."

"It wasn't no picnic for me either," Pastor Cornbread interjected.

"We use to fight like cats and dogs but somehow by the grace of God we always managed to work things out. Pastor Cornbread use to have muscles like Mr. Olympia. Look at him now," she said as she rubbed his stomach which hung over his pants. "He looks like a pot roast with all the trimmings." As the congregation focused their eyes on him, he tried to suck his belly in. The congregation laughed.

She smiled and continued. "I use to be able to run my fingers through his curly hair, but now he has a sunroof top. I'm praying God will restore him to his former glory." She patted him on his bald head. "But I want to tell you one thing, I wouldn't take nothing for my journey."

Pastor Cornbread grabbed the microphone from her before she had a chance to add more. "Okay, that's enough honey. Once you start her to talking she never knows when to quit." The congregation chuckled. "Sister Cornbread and I have been happily married for over forty years. "Marriage is a beautiful thing and our love has grown for each other more and more. I feel so comfortable with the girl that I can even pop my toes without her complaining. Now that's love."

"Pudd'n you're right. Why complaining is not even in our vocabulary," said Emma.

"Thank you honey," said Pastor Cornbread as he kissed her on her cheek and she took her seat. Then he began the ceremony. "Now, who gives these women to these men."

"I do," said Uncle Joedale. He raised each of their veils, kissed each one the cheek, turned around and took his seat beside Aunt Pauline.

"Is this a wedding or a retirement home party," sneered T-Bone as he hunched Cleo and laughed. "I'm sure if Pastor Cornbread knew that marriage was going to be like that, he probably would have bought an electric blanket instead. Adam started all this marriage stuff. I'm sure if he knew what type of wife Eve turned out to be he would have asked God for his rib back."

"Hush, T-Bone," said Cleo. "I can't hear the ceremony."

"Do you, Brother Riley?" asked Pastor Cornbread.

"Yes, sir," said Riley.

"Wait till I ask you the question first." Riley along with the congregation started laughing.

"Do you, Riley, promise before God and man to take this woman, forever and ever and I do mean ever, till . . . Jesus comes and get us in the rapture? In other words, she's yours for keeps and you can't bring her back."

"Well, Pastor that's a long time. Let me think about it a minute." Just then Olivia punched him in his side with her fist. "Ouch! I mean I do," said Riley as he rubbed his sore ribs with his hand.

"Do you take her as your awfully, I mean lawfully wedded wife? Will you hold her. Will you squeeze her?" he asked as he cleared his throat.

"Well, that's what the honeymoon is for," said Riley as he smiled and Olivia blushed.

"In plenty and in want? In joy and sorrow? In sickness and in health?"

"Yes, I do."

Then Pastor Cornbread turned and addressed Olivia. "Olivia, do you promise before God and man to take this man as your husband to love, cherish him as long as you both shall live? In plenty and want? In joy and sorrow? In sickness and health? Do you promise to honor and obey?"

"Obey?" questioned Francis. "I'm going to take that part out of my wedding vows. I'm not obeying nobody."

"I promise to try," said Olivia. Riley looked over at her. "I mean of course I do."

"Now for the next couple. Do you Brother Isaac, promise before God and man to take Georgia Mae, forever and ever? In plenty and in want? In joy and in sorrow? In sickness and in health?"

"Well, yes I do."

Then Pastor Cornbread turned and addressed Georgia. "Do you Georgia Mae take Isaac as your lawfully wedded husband?"

"Yes, yes."

"Do you promise to cherish him as long as you both shall live? In plenty and want? In joy and sorrow? In sickness and health?"

"I promise," said Georgia cheerfully.

He posed the question, "Do you promise to honor and obey even if it means cooking, washing and ironing?"

"Yes," she continued, "I love to cook and do house work."

"Some women don't like to do stuff like that." He stared over at Emma as a hint.

"Is there anyone that object to why these two couples can not be joined together in holy matrimony?

Let them speak now or forever hold their peace," Pastor Cornbread firmly stated.

Aunt Pauline held up her wrinkled arm.

Pastor Cornbread, acknowledging her, "Yes ma'am. What do you object too?"

"I don't mind Riley marrying Olivia that boy is a saint. But I don't want Georgia to marry Isaac.

"Why?"

"I object because he's a heathen. When I first met him I knew he wasn't the man for my precious Georgia. He insulted me when he came to ask for Georgia's hand in marriage. I should have slapped him up side his head for that, but I'm a lady."

"Is that true, Brother Isaac?"

"Pastor I have tried to apologize to her many times but every time I called her on the telephone she would hang up on me."

"Sister Pauline?" questioned Pastor Cornbread, "You didn't?"

"Maybe," she admitted with a guilty look on her face.

"Sister Pauline, you have to accept his apology if he asked you to forgive him. I'm sure he didn't mean to insult you. Did you, Brother Isaac?"

"No sir."

As a goodwill gesture, Isaac walked over to her and gave her a kiss on her cheek.

She quickly took her satin dress sleeve and wiped it off as she felt both embarrassed and ashamed of her attitude towards him. "Now don't be slobbering all over folks."

"Do you forgive me?"

"Okay, okay. I forgive you. Well Pastor, what ya waiting for? I suggest you carry on if you want to be paid for this service."

"Who has the rings?" After no one responded he asked the question again. "I said, who has the rings?"

Smiling proudly Uncle Bunt jumped up from his seat and walked to the altar. "I do," he answered as he searched in his pockets.

"I told you Bunt to put those rings in a place you would not forget them," said Pauline as she rolled her eyes and folded her arms.

"Hold your horses, I've got 'em in my secret compartment." He reached down and took his right shoe and pulled off his sock. The smell of corn chips was released into the air. He had even had his toes polished for the occasion. There they were two large diamond rings on his middle toe. He pulled the rings off and handed them to Pastor Cornbread. The smell of his sweaty feet was still circulating in the air.

"Oh no!" yelled Aunt Pauline as she made her way towards him with her cane. "I hope your life insurance is paid up because I am about to cash yours in."

"Hold up, Pauline," said Uncle Bunt as he hopped around on one leg as he tried to put his sock back on. "My feet are clean woman. I took a bath before I put those rings on my toes."

She managed to whack him across his foot.

"Ouch!" Uncle Bunt hollered out.

"Calm down, Aunt Pauline," requested Riley as he grabbed her arm. "This is my wedding day and I want to get this over so I can get the honeymoon on the road."

"I tell you one thing, their fingers better not turn green."

Pastor Cornbread turned to the grooms and handed each a beautiful custom designed ring. "These rings are symbols of your union together that must never be broken. Gentlemen, take their left hand and repeat after me. With this ring, I do wed and give it to thee for a token and pledge of my constant love for and faith in you and God."

The men took the rings repeated after Pastor Cornbread, and slid it on their bride's finger. "As you put this ring on her finger, remember that this is a symbol of you love and never ending promise to take care of her."

"By the power of God, Jesus Christ, the Holy Spirit, the State of Texas, Abundant Love Church, by the power of these here lights, by the power of the Deacon Board, the Board of Elders, the Youth Department . . ."

Riley turned to Isaac and whispered, "If he keep this up we'll gonna be too old to have children." They both giggled.

"The one you will have till we'll caught up in the rapture," Pastor Cornbread continued. "Till the sky burst wide open and Jesus steps out the cloud. And you hear the trumpet sound. And angels will be singing glory hallelujah to the Lord. I said I want to be in that great day."

"Preach boy!" shouted Aunt Pauline as she stood to her feet and began to clap her hands.

He came to himself as he noticed the look on Riley's face. "Oh," clearing his throat, "I'm sorry, I was caught up there for a moment. When you and Sister Olivia have fights you can't be calling your Aunt Pauline, Uncle Joedale, or Uncle Bunt to solve them. What I really want to say is every tub has gotta sit on it's own bottom."

"That's right!" added Joedale. "Don't be calling me once you leave the nest you're on your own."

Pastor Cornbread raised both hands in the air and spoke a blessing over each couple. Then he concluded with, "I now pronounce you, Riley and Olivia, man and wife in the name of the Father, and of the Son, and of the Holy Ghost. I now pronounce you, Isaac and Georgia, man and wife in the name of the Father, and of the Son, and of the Holy Ghost. And in the words of my favorite movie star Mr. Spock, 'Live long and prosper.' You may kiss your newborn brides."

"Kiss those women!" the audience shouted in unison.

They quickly grabbed their brides and planted a good long kiss on them as the onlookers awed. The audience applauded.

"Wow!" declared Olivia and Georgia as they grabbed the men for another sample. The sanctuary thundered with applause once again.

Uncle Joedale slapped his hand down on his knee. "That's what I'm talking about." Then he yelled out, "Fellows if that didn't light you're fire your wood is wet!"

"Now go be fruitful and multiply," said Pastor Cornbread as he patted Riley and Isaac on the back. Laughter could be hear coming from the congregation.

Then the single women shouted out with a great anticipation, "Throw the bouquet! Throw the bouquet! Throw the bouquet!"

Olivia and Georgia tied the two bouquets together with a piece of ribbon. They agreed to throw it together. So they turned around backwards and made ready to grant their request. The women, including a few of the married ones, and the Board of Elders huddled together into football formation mediating on their strategy for catching the bouquet.

"See this is the place you can find out who is desperate and ready to get married. The woman who leaps over the others or slides in, that's the one I'm going to asked out for a date," T-Bone replied.

"What happens to women after the bouquet is thrown?" asked Coach Parker.

"I don't know man but their whole personality changes when it comes to those flowers," T-Bone replied.

Just as predicted, as the bouquet were flying though the air, the women went wild. They pushed and shoved each other out of the way.

Coach Parker picked up his ink pen and pretended like it was a microphone as he began to do a play-by-play announcement. "Now Old Lady Andrews catches bouquet. She is off to a slow start. I don't believe she's going to make it. Oh no, she was tackled at the twentieth pew by a Misty Lewis." Coach paused, "Old Lady Andrews is not getting up. She may be out all season."

"Misty has just stripped the bouquet from her hands. It looks like she is going all the way. She sprints to the thirty, now to the twenty-five, twenty, fifteen. Oh no! Misty has just fumbles the bouquet at the fifteenth pew. It is recovered by Peaches Norwood!"

"That's a woman I wouldn't mine taking out," T-Bone told Coach as he watched the action intensify.

Peaches is tackled by a pack of desperate women that seem to come out of nowhere. "Looks like the Calhoun family is pulling the crowd of women off of the top of Peaches as a goodwill gesture. We can only see who's in possession of them after the dust clears. One of the Calhoun sisters has just grabbed the bouquet. It's Jenny Calhoun. Looks like she's going for the power sweep as the rest of the Calhoun clan run interference." She looks around and spots her sister, Little Biscuit, down at the altar. Jenny rares her arm back she made ready for a long pass. "I not sure but looks like she is going for a 'Hail Mary.' She is. But wait, here comes Sister Lulu up from the rear."

"I hope she doesn't get it. I'll never get rid of her now."

T-Bone knew, even as he waited for the result, that he was a doomed man. Doomed, doomed, doomed. Doomed like a convicted felon with a life sentence. All hope gone of ever getting rid of Lulu was apparent by his tone.

Lulu intercepted the bouquet and dove for the altar.

"She's . . . she's safe!" said Coach Parker with excitement as he swung his hands out like a referee giving the safe sign.

"I can't believe it!" said T-Bone. "I just can't believe it."

"That's has got to the be play of the day," said Coach Parker.

Lulu sprang to her feet immediately and faced the group of men where T-Bone was standing. "Guess who's getting married next?"

He glanced over at her and shouted back, "Not me!"

Cleo shook his head and sighed. "That was the most shameless display of womanhood I have every seen."

"Well, I don't see what's wrong with it. Kind of reminds ya of a football game with no rules don't it Coach," said T-Bone.

"If I had another bouquet I would throw it out there," added Coach Parker. "I need to get some of these woman to try out for football next spring. Boy, I learned ten new plays just watching 'em."

The single women began to pick up piece of flowers, leaves, and stems from off of the floor to save as mementoes and hurried off to hunt down the single men.

T-Bone shook his head and laughed as a gang of about fifty women rushed over towards them. "Ladies he told them, "Me and my friend are like two small fish and five loaves of bread. What are we among so many? I believe I saw at least sixty single men rush out of the sanctuary. If you hurry you probably could catch them." As he was talking, the women dashed out of the church heading for the parking lot.

"Thanks, T-Bone. That was close. By the way, I wonder where that young lady went?" asked Cleo as he looked around. I hope she didn't leave."

"I'm sure she's around here somewhere." He placed his hand on Cleo's shoulder. "Let's go over and kiss the brides."

They walked over to where the newlyweds were standing. "Well, congratulations Old Man Riley and Mr. Isaac," said T-Bone as he shook each of their hands.

"I'm a blessed man," said Riley.

"Me too," said Isaac. I want you to meet our wives. He introduced and pointed to each one. "Olivia and Georgia, this is T-Bone, Coach Parker, and Cleo. Good friends of ours."

The men kissed Olivia and Georgia on the cheek.

"You must be the gang from the barbershop," Olivia stated as the men nodded. "Well, we're glad to meet all of you."

"Excuse us honey but Isaac and I have some financial business to take care of with Pastor Cornbread," said Riley. "We'll be back as soon as we can so we can leave for the reception."

"I'll go with you," requested Coach as the three of them walked off together.

"Which one of you is Riley's barber?"

"That would be him," T-Bone pointed to Cleo.

"Thank you so much young man. Riley's hair looks really nice today." I'm, glad you took that love curl mess of his hair. I just don't know what got into him that day."

"Yes ma'am you are so right. It made him look like a old goat didn't it," added T-Bone as he laughed.

"Well," Olivia replied softly. "Just say it did not bring out his best features."

"Well, how does it feel to be married?" Cleo asked as he changed the subject of the conversation.

"Just wonderful child,"responded Olivia. "Are you fellows married?"

"No ma'am. Both T-Bone and I are single."

"Yeah," stated T-Bone, putting his hands in his front pant pockets, "I'm going to keeping it that way."

"You might feel different if he met our hair dresser," said Olivia. She'll a really knock out."

"Mmm-hmmm. That's right and she's a nice Christian young lady," Georgia added as Barbara Ann appeared. "This is Barbara Ann everybody, our hair dresser . . . I mean our hair stylist," she said proudly as she gave her a hug. "She's beautiful isn't she fellows?"

The men agreed which was evident by the expression on each of their faces.

"Oh, Mother Georgia," Barbara Ann blushed as she hear the comment. She stood beside Georgia and smiled graciously at the group. "Hello, glad to meet everyone," she said as she extended her hand.

Cleo's hand begin shake and his voice trembled as he stretched out his hand to shake hers. "My name is C-C-C-Cleo." He found himself mesmerized by her eyes and noticed T-Bone was not immune to their effect, either.

"I'm T-T-T-T-Bone."

"Hello Cleo and T-Bone," she spoke softly.

Georgia was determined not to let this opportunity pass her by to play matchmaker. "Barbara Ann, Cleo runs the barbershop," she said as her skills kicked into action. "I bet you two have lots in common since both of you'll are in the hair business," Georgia said. "I know what, why don't the two of you come over for dinner next Sunday after church."

"That's a wonderful idea," add Olivia, "Georgia's a wonderful cook."

"I would like that," T-Bone said as he smiled at Barbara Ann.

"Not you son, I meant Cleo."

"Yes ma'am I would be honored," said Cleo as he accepted the invitation.

"Me to," Barbara Ann replied as she blushed again.

About that time, Riley, Isaac, and Coach Parker returned. "Are you ladies ready to go?" Riley asked as he reached over and kissed Olivia on the cheek.

"We're ready," Olivia said as she smiled.

"We will meet ya'll at the reception," said Cleo as he, T-Bone, and Coach Parker shook their hands and left.

"I sure could use a cup of coffee right about now," said Olivia as they started walking towards the front of the church.

"Me too," said Georgia. "But I'm usually the one that's fixing it."

"Not any more," said Isaac as he took her hand and held it. "Me and Riley love to cook and from now on you ladies are going to have breakfast in bed every morning."

"That will be wonderful," replied Georgia. "I like being married already."

As they walked from the sanctuary the ladies had gathered outside and tossed rose petals as they made their way to the Love Mobile. Riley had it beautifully restored and ready for action.

Three Years Later

It was a nice Spring day as the two couples sat on the front porch having a cup of coffee. As they sat in a white wicker love seat Olivia laid her head back on Riley's chest.

Georgia and Isaac were in the porch swing, snuggled up close to each other. She was giggling and hunching up her shoulders as he gently blew in her ear and kissed her on her neck. "Isaac you are so silly," she whispered to him.

As they were enjoying their time with each other Lulu rushed across the street, into the yard, and up onto the porch. "Good morning everybody."

"Good morning," they replied back.

"Did you hear the news?" she asked as her eyes gleamed with joy.

"What news?" questioned Olivia as she sat up.

"Cleo and Francis are getting married."

"Why, I just knew it," exclaimed Olivia. "They were just made for each other. There has been so many weddings at the church lately I can hardly keep up."

"Well if they're as happy as we are that's a blessing," Riley said as he turned and kissed Olivia on the check.

"Would you like a cup of coffee dear?" asked Georgia as she made ready to pour her a cup.

"No ma'am I've got a date."

"Well Lulu, good for you," commented Olivia.

"I can't believe how much my life has changed after I joined Pastor Willis' church."

"Ours too baby," stated Georgia. "After we changed membership it's like we are new people."

"I have you all to thank for it because remember what Pastor Cornbread said during the wedding about how a man don't like a woman to chase him. After his messages I always felt condemned. But when Pastor Willis preached it, I really understood what God meant. It was as years of baggage fell off of me. For the first time in my life I realized that I was a beauty person inside and out. So I started concentrating on what God wanted me to achieve in my life. No more jumbo curlers and big house shoes for me. Can you tell that I've lost over sixty pounds?"

"You sure have baby. You look good too," expressed Georgia as she eyed her from head to toe. "Who is this fortunate young man?"

Surprising to all she said proudly, "Winford."

"You mean T-Bone?" questioned Riley.

"That's right. The one and only."

As they were talking T-Bone drove up to her house.

"Well, got to go," said Lulu as she headed down the steps and back across the street.

After T-Bone spotted her coming across the street, he hopped out of the car, ran around to the other side, and opened the door for her to get in. He waved to a stunned audience as he rushed back to the driver's side, got in and drove off.

"That's a miracle," replied Isaac. "Boy that T-Bone has really changed."

Olivia took a sip of coffee from her cup. "We all have changed. I've learned that life is to be enjoyed. It's too short to be miserable."

"Yeah," added Georgia as she lifted her cup to her lips. "Like mama use to say, 'We've all finally woke up and smelled the coffee.'"

Ya'll Come on Down and Visit Sunnydale, Ya'll Hear!

Let Sister Thelma Johnson take you to a whole new level in the spiritual experience. That Sister Johnson is a mess I tell you. As the pastor's wife she rules and reigns at Sunnydale. What is she up to now is guaranteed to bring a non stop laughter if you stop by for a visit. She's a tuff old gal that takes no stuff off of nobody. "The best relationships are formed when you do it my way!" Thelma said. A must read book, *"A Church with Spots and Wrinkles,"* by Deborah Elum, 5 ½ x 8 ½, 100 page trade book, ISBN 0-7392-0123-9, $10.00.

Have You Experienced Dreams and Visions from God?

Includes a foreward by best-selling author Mary K. Baxter, author of "A Divine Revelation of Hell." Norma Powers Marlowe knows that many people all over the world have experienced dreams and visions from God. He uses these experiences to illuminate one's mind and write unforgettable words about Himself on the tablet of one's heart.

When Norma started having visions, it was as if God was opening a book. Each page contained more wisdom, knowledge, and revelation of how awesome He is. Even as she tell you about these glorious experiences, they burn within your heart. It is her prayer that her experiences will stir up a passion in you that you too will declare His glory.

Norma Powers Marlowe is a talented author, music composer, and singer. Her kindness and generosity extends out to many people in ministry. Many guests have visited or stayed in her home, such as Ruth Ward Heflin, Silvania Machado, Mary K. Baxter, and many others from around the world. "Heaven Declares His Glory," by Norma Powers Marlowe, 5 ½ x 8 ½, 100 page trade book, ISBN 0-9679441-3-9, $10.00.